*(Searching for Miss Poole)*

# In Unlikely Places

### by

### ReBecca Béguin

*(Searching for Miss Poole)*

# In Unlikely Places

by

**ReBecca Béguin**

**New Victoria Publishers, Inc.**

ISBN  0-934678-25-1



**Library of Congress Cataloging-in-Publication Data**
Béguin, ReBecca.
   (Searching for Miss Poole) In Unlikely Places/ by ReBecca Béguin.
      p.      cm.
   ISBN 0-934678-25-1  :  $8.95
      1. Africa--History--19th century--Fiction. 2. British--Africa--History--19th century--Fiction. I. Title  II. Title: In Unlikely Places.
   PS3552. E274S4 1990
   813'.54--dc20
                                                    90-5940
                                                    CIP

*For Holly*

# Introduction

That I realized my lesbian identity early on was never a big deal for me; it was a matter of fact like my height, hair, eye or skin color. To deny it was impossible. If it helped shaped my sense of alienation in the world, so what was new? I could point much more readily to other contributing factors which I sought to find peace with in myself. Much harder for me was coming to terms with being born of missionaries in South Africa, being of Africa and not of Africa. No matter how strong the bond for me, the gift of my time there was finite.

I have been through the accursed feeling of discovering that missionary movements anywhere at any time are an arm of colonialism. I also understand that the church, in another context, can offer sanctuary and a window towards liberation. I believe my parents went to Africa with the latter view in mind, and with them I crossed boundaries the majority of whites did not dream of nor condone. This also made life complicated, and ultimately constricting. On a simple, true level, what made sense was the sacred space under an ancient tree which had shaded black tribal gatherings and before them, all manner of wild game; or it was catching the last glimpses of a vast, wild, and stunningly beautiful land being quickly, relentlessly, and harshly divided, its people scattered and broken.

My family came back to the States on the threshold of the seventies, when the stage was set for extreme turmoil in South Africa—the vise had been tightened ever since I had witnessed Britain turn over the government to independent, white rule. When we returned here, this nation's preoccupation was with Vietnam, and I had to use a map to explain where I had come from and what it was like there.

But then things came bluntly in the open at last, and I too, have been able to grapple with the conflicts and winds of change in South Africa—here, from afar, so far. And at last, it is a more optimistic feeling.

If I write, it is to go back into—or it comes out of—my dream-time. If I spin a folk-tale, I hope to capture essences out of respect and love; to honor explorers like Mary Kingsley who went to Africa in defiance of the conventions of her time, and in her rare example, with strong anti-colonialist sentiments. Also, to remember and celebrate the strong black tribal woman, particularly of sub-Saharan cultures, whose stories became lost as oral traditions broke down. Many other European women also went off to Africa on their own—the first tended to be missionaries—but why, really?—others as artists, naturalists, teachers, yes, and trophy-hunters. They were visionaries, individualists and eccentrics.

If I write 'history,' it is metaphor. I do not wish to recreate any particular biography, but to test some core discussions that come out of my own struggle with reality. I do not profess to be an anthropologist, correct in all detail. I admit to poetic license, and my scenes are pure fiction. This is a story about Africa, because at my root depth, it is Africa I love—yet I do not assume to write it as anything but a European. And always in search of wholeness.

# 1.  1895, Equatorial West Africa

Lily gazed across the great expanse of black swamp, smooth as obsidian. The vast, muddy stretches were broken only by islands of tall, sharp elephant-grass in bold emerald greens. "It's going to be one hell of a picnic," she announced to herself aloud and in English.

Her Faung porters, their bronze skins gleaming with sweat, were in a palaver of their own—sharp clicks of their tongues in disgust at the sight before them. The lead porter, Mbo, waved his long bangled arms and pointed with his scythe of beaten metal matter-of-factly. The others, all four of them, put down their burdens, squatting as they deliberated. One of them lit up a clay pipe that Lily had given them at the start of the expedition.

Lily stood waiting, the long sleeves of her shirt sticking to her skin; her cotton pin-striped skirt clung about her legs; strands of dark hair were plastered down her cheeks.

Before them lay a most authentic African swamp—swamp as far as they could see. Torpid waves of heat hung across the surface of the mud, and the evaporating water brought with it the unavoidable, rich smell of rotting vegetation. Undoubtedly, elephants would come to wallow in such a place for a holiday and think they were in paradise.

Lily pulled on the brim of her cloth hat to shade her eyes from the hot tropical sun, beginning to regret that they had emerged from the dark canopy of the rain forest. She might as well be standing on the edge of a desert.

Mbo broke away from the debate with his companions, stuck a foot in the murky water. His leg disappeared up to the knee. He spat and nodded his head.

1

"Wonderful," commented Lily tersely in English, brushing away flies that were aiming for her eyes, and trying to ignore the mosquitoes, "a bottomless swamp. Isn't there any way around it?" She gestured with her hands in circles that spoke for her much better than if she had spoken in her awkward Faung.

"No, Ma." Mbo said in the pidgin English he had picked up from traders and missionaries .

"Crocodiles?"

"No, crocs, Ma."

"Oh good." She sighed in relief. The water wasn't fresh enough. Even crocodiles had their standards.

Then for her benefit he sucked in his cheeks, his lips puckered like a fish's and he made sharp sucking noises. Lily looked at him blankly but the others took up the discussion in renewed animation. The one she called Peta in her poor attempt to make the appropriate sound of his name, held out a muddy hand he had dipped in the muck. On his arm hung an ugly, elongated slug.

"Leeches!" exclaimed Lily. Tick infestations were one thing—she had grown accustomed to them at any rate—but leeches?

Mbo, without further ado, stripped off his loin cloth and wrapped it around his neck. He pulled on the end of Lily's sash, indicating that she wrap it around her neck. He pointed to her jugular vein, and signed by way of explanation, that this way she would not grow dizzy from loss of blood.

"A scarf in the middle of the tropics? I left that convention back in the fogs of London. But that's as far as I'll go...."

All the other porters prepared themselves in the same fashion as Mbo, taking up their bundles once again.

Lily clutched her canvas portmanteau, full of secret and precious contents that only she would ever miss. The bag held all her field notes, her pens, her paints and brushes, diary and sheets of rice paper. Wrapped in layers of canvas deep within the center were all her completed illustrations of plant specimens. There too, lay her letter of introduction to Miss Margery Poole, if she ever found her. She carried this bundle on top of her head when she had to. She would carry it that way through the swamp, watch every step.

She watched Mbo as he led the way into the muddy water feeling around with a long staff. First his knees disappeared, then his thighs, his waist, until the water reached the center of his chest. He turned his face back to beam triumphantly.

She bit her lip in agitation while tying her sash securely around her neck, and placing the well-oiled revolver she had kept at her waist into her bag. It looked more likely that they would have to swim than walk.

Masa, the porter carrying the talking-drum, was careful to have it high atop his head, along with the pack of her trade goods that he carried, as high and as tenderly placed as her portmanteau. His drum was vital to their communication.

Hitching up her skirt, Lily stepped forward. One by one her black, leather boots disappeared into the mud, followed by her legs, sheathed as they were in white pantaloons. Her skirt ballooned out as she sank to her waist, her feet finding nothing solid yet. She tucked it around her waist, out of the way. She was barely able to move forward with the gooey water almost tickling her under her chin, glad for the function of her sash at her neck-protection against the leeches.

There they were—four brown heads in front of her, and then, the last porter to her rear.

Mbo led them gingerly, circuitously, feeling constantly for some sort of footing. He grinned in triumph when they found more shallow ground. Slogging their way hip deep was much better, but every so often, they'd hit another deep spot and flounder.

Now and again they'd stop on the islands of grass, the blades cutting their palms, to dislodge any leeches they had picked up. They zigzagged east, then west, not the bee-line due north Lily had hoped for. She had no idea of how accurate Mbo was. She simply had to trust and follow.

She lost track of time as the sun began its descent. Her pantaloons were pushed up against her thighs and she could feel the pressure of the mud in her boots. Yes, it was unpleasant but it didn't hurt. It was gruelling under the sun, but where was anything she could call pain? Did her head reel from the heat, the stench, or the leeches sucking out her blood? As was her way, she retreated to a place deep within.

No, pain belonged in another place. It was something that had ached in her joints in a dark, dank house back in England. Pain was being bound by duty without question; trying to revive her mother with smelling salts yet again; running into the cold, pelting rain at midnight to fetch the doctor one more time. Pain was reading the musty books from her long-absent father's library by candle-light as she attended her mother through the interminable nights and in knowing from those books that there were places and people she was denied. The pain had been in the longing and the despair—in knowing that there were sunny, sweltering climates, mountain ranges and jungles that English people could see, write about, even die in, while she sat, enveloped by shadow and the smell of sickness. Pain had been in wondering, why can't I go too?—in feeling that she would rather drop dead from fever on the equator than die a slow death in England.

Sometimes to hold back the shadows, she had read aloud even after her mother had started her incoherent mumblings in her sleep: ...*and traders may rely on steamers up the Oguye River as far as Fitzpatrick Pool, created long ago by a huge volcanic eruption which collapsed into itself, and further, the Greely Mission on the English side. Beyond the Rapids, one can only proceed by river canoe, a treacherous balancing act, while one must also employ native paddlers to keep the canoe away from rocks and crocodiles.*

*'It is not advised to proceed beyond the mission....'*

Not advised to proceed. "Indeed!" she had announced, "then that is where I must go, mustn't I, mother?"

Invariably, her mother would sink into a rhythmic, all pervasive snore which seemed to echo in Lily's ears dully—*Not advised to proceed, not advised to proceed.*

Mbo found them an island—a mud-covered outcropping of rock as big as a hippo's back. They crawled out there, carefully peeling off leeches, and taking a drink from a pouch made of goat-stomach. With mud-caked hands they portioned out dried fish and plantain cakes. Nothing tasted good, and fanning herself with her hat, Lily wondered how long it would take for her body to rebuild the blood supply she had lost to leeches over the hours. Her body ached from pushing through the pressure of the mud and water; her head throbbed.

She needn't have worried about the blood loss if she followed Mbo's example. He ate the leeches he took off his body, cajoling her to do the same, talking to her in Faung. "It has your blood in it. You must put it back in your body." As always in the way he taught her, his hands were in motion, his face entreating. She had flung four leeches into the mud, pinching each wound on her body closed. She watched him as he prepared the slug by sliding his fingers down its sides to squeeze the mud off, then chopping off the mouth. Head thrown back, he plopped the leech down the back of his throat, gulping it like a heron. She doubted that she could make her throat do that, but eyed the last leech, clamped on her shoulder. Pinching its mouth with his fingers so that it let go, he cleaned and cut it for her. There was blood, all right, as much as a good swarm of mosquitoes might get all together over the course of an insufferable colonial dinner down on the coast. Put the blood back in. She tossed her head back, shut her eyes and plopped the leech in, thinking to gag, but amazingly, it slippped down her throat without gagging her.

She gazed back across swamp, the distant rain forest were almost too dim to make out anymore. Turning north, she wanted to believe, yes, that she could distinguish distant trees, solid land. She had peered and peered in the same way when a boat had rocked under her feet, waiting to come upon the coast of Africa, waiting to witness the forest rising out from the sea.

\* \* \*

It had been then, almost within the first moment she had set eyes on what was to become her beloved Africa, that she had also heard the name 'Margery Poole.' The captain came to talk to her on deck, requesting her to deliver letters to the remote English mission which was to be her eventual destination.

At the start of the voyage she had been put off by his face,

5

red from too much sun and liquor, puffy from too much salt in his diet. But he had proved to be unobtrusively informative with his dry humor, "fever humor," he called it. He had grown jaded long ago, from taking aboard too many fever-stricken Europeans for their journey home only to have to bury them at sea. He had a new fever story for her every night at dinner. 'A fellow came out to the Equator,' he'd say, 'to make his fortune in minerals. Ah, but he should have gone further south for that, all he got was the fever. Brought his coffin on board with him—full of booze.'

"And it is doubtful, Miss Bascombe," he had said with a scowl from beneath his greasy cap, tapping the letters, "that these can possibly reach the intended reader." She had read the name he pointed to with his swollen fingers, Miss Margery Poole. She almost expected the name to be a geographic location rather than a person. "Why?" she felt compelled to inquire.

He had smiled then as if he had asked many an adventurer to do the same task for him without success. He spoke mysteriously. "She hasn't been seen for years, ever since she came back from her furlough. Some say she cracked when she went back to England, that she'd gone 'too bush' and couldn't handle crossing a street—simply too dumbfounded even to talk. I'd say she was about your age when she came back out. Wouldn't you know but she moved her mission off somewhere, took off into the jungle and went native without so much as a 'how d' you do' to her sponsors. She could be dead from the fever by now. No one knows. The church hasn't been able to give her her stipend, can't even send her her ration of tea! Both of which I am giving into your charge."

"Well," Lily had said, pocketing the bundle of letters, "if she is alive, I swear I shall find her, for I intend to trade in the interior. Perhaps, I shall find out what has become of her at last."

"Then allow me to give you a letter of introduction," said Captain Lowell, reminding her of his office as representative of the crown in the absence of any other to fill the post. "And don't trade away all your tobacco; save some for her. She strolled the decks with me most every evening when we were at sea that last time, don't you know, and smoked a small pipe. Said it helped give her sea legs."

Lily had been able to tell from the tone he used that he was testing to see whether she was shocked at this detail. He had seemed satisfied to find she was not; nodded in approval of her. Is that why he had cultivated a friendship with her this voyage, inviting her to the captain's table each dinner? Was it to size her up for this mission? "Yes, if anyone were to find her, it would be you," he had said, adding, "D'you know—I didn't find her as daft as all that. It was just England that didn't agree with her. When she said good-bye to me, I knew she would not come back."

* * *

Now Lily stood exhausted and covered in black mud, her neck stiff from the load atop her head. Perhaps she was the one to try and find Margery Poole but, so far, that woman remained as much a mirage as the hope of solid footing for the moment. How odd that these Faung men can emerge from the swamp as though dressed in a new skin, she marvelled, while I look like a filthy, unwrung mop. She had never understood so completely before how unnecessary, in the name of civilization, clothes could be.

Yet she proceeded, head held high, not in any attempt at dignity in the name of her race or gender, no, not even for the name Bascombe, but because her nose was trying in vain to find some relief from the stench.

How many bodies of water had she come across that she had wanted to name for this legendary woman, Margery Poole?—like Fitzpatrick might have had the gall to do on his maps. And yet, she always held out for some better prospect. As she slogged along she wondered whether she had found that very body of water worthy of the name. Surely she had met a match here.

But the point now was not to feel doomed. Do not feel doomed; she had taken on that attitude in conscious exercise while still at her mother's sickbed and while waiting down the years for release—while blowing dust off her father's books.

7

Africa had become a distinctive shape in her mind over the years, and Clive Fitzpatrick's book, *Expeditions into Africa*, from the 1860s was her bible. Not that she didn't question his point of view on almost every subject he covered. She had memorized many passages simply in the hunger of her rereading.

*The naming of Africa is essential to the cartographer, as we wrench meaningful names out of the dark, impossible clutches of savage tongue, thereby taming treacherous passages, rendering them passable.* He had written and failed to add—*if only on paper.* Why?—out of smugness, perhaps, that he had made his way, undaunted, undefeated. She shook her head time and again over his *naming and taming.* Would her passage through the swamp be any easier if she were to call it Margery Poole, rather than by some Faung version which probably meant *where elephant trample and mortals fear to tread?* Was the Oguye River any less full of crocodiles if called by the name, Pursey—after the general—as Fitzpatrick would have had it? Did any less Europeans die from the fever by calling it malaria?

She had tried to meet with Fitzpatrick in the early stages of her scheming and planning, writing a letter of introduction for herself, mentioning her father's contacts. A letter had come back: What? A woman wanting to trade in the interior of French Congo and Bradding's territory on the Equator? Utter nonsense.

Utter nonsense. *Not advised to proceed.* How long had that response set her back—months—before she found her spirit? Of course, part of the lag in time was due to her brother's inability to make his own travel plans.

Then one day she had read from Fitzpatrick's book again and had been astonished to realize he must be wrong about things. She began to pick apart Fitzpatrick's ultimate authority on how to mount an expedition: *No less than fifteen porters are required on any foray. Five to carry food, five to carry the camping essentials—tent, rubber and canvas bath, kitchen and dining equipment, silver set etc., and five to carry field gear—ammunition, guns, surveying tools, camera and plates, not to forget personal gear, clothes and trade items.*

So, forget the silver set! she had scoffed, forget the rubber bath, the camera, its tripod and plates. Eat local fare in local fashion, likewise, sleep. I shall do with no more than five porters, carry a pistol and call it done. As far as surveying equipment, she had his maps didn't she?—neatly cut out of his book and kept in her portmanteau—and a compass.

The sun was sinking fast when the five porters and a light-headed Lily finally 'came ashore.' First they had to wade up and over many fallen, slippery trees, but at least it was only waist-deep, hard as it was to keep bundles balanced.

They set up camp on a bank of rocks which were dry and free of mud. By way of making camp, a fire was lit, sparks flying into the darkening sky as monkeys screeched in the forest. Peta, Mbo and the others went hunting.

Lily had the world to herself as she undressed, one item at a time, finding clean clothes in one of the bundles. There was no clean water to wash with, but at least she was dry, the dirty mop of her clothes spread out on the hot rocks.

She sat down by the fire to contemplate the next day's route, re-drawing her own map from what she had found out, compared to what Fitzpatrick had recorded. True, he had charted out marsh, but had mentioned log pathways that rubber-plant harvesters built. It was obvious that she had found a more eastern end to his marsh, the muddy end. His portrayal of crocodile infestation and boggy pits were either a work of his imagination, or else the swamp had fresh water entering it farther along where he had gone. She knew it was useless to say she had followed his course precisely, because she wasn't certain she had. It was not as though he had left signs though he had clearly drawn a border between the French and English territories.

Which side of his imaginary line was she on? Was she within the 'safe realms' of English jurisdiction again. The idea amused her so that she laughed aloud, a throaty croak. I'm as good as lost, she crooned at the glow of the fire, its tongue of flame licking the rocks.

She might have become forlorn then,but heard the calls of the returning hunters, a song of happiness at their good fortune—*we have brought the meat, we have brought the game down; we have brought the meat, with our cleverness and skill we have brought it down*—three small antelope which Mbo held up on his spear like so many fish out of the river.

The men set to work skinning the animals, a task she had finally grown accustomed to watching without flinching. How deftly their hands moved with their flint knives, slicing skin away from flesh. Setting up a spit, they passed the gourd of beer around.

And as Lily said every evening: "Perhaps tomorrow I will find Miss P."

\* \* \*

A mighty sound rent the air, deep and primal from the very belly of the ancestors. Lily sat up stiffly, shaken out of sleep at the terrible sound.

Nearby Mbo was already up, squatting on his blanket, his head cocked in deep interest, waiting.

Once again the sound boomed and echoed above the forest which seemed to resonate. Mbo caught her glance and broke into a wide smile.

A lion's roar, yes most certainly a lion's roar, thought Lily, rousing to the damp dawn, Mbo already stirring up the embers of the fire. A lion! That could mean only one thing— open land nearby. She consulted eagerly with Mbo. Yes, indeed, Ma, a lion roared from the open escarpment above them. They would have to climb today but he had already scouted out the game paths.

Eagerly she consulted her map. She was on course, close enough anyway. A wide plateau was all that separated her now from the Robolo River with its deep ravines and boiling rapids. She could almost hear the rush of water in her mind or perhaps it was that her ears were still full of the sound of the upper Oguye which she had left behind almost frantically, her idea to search for Miss P suddenly urgent.

\* \* \*

Things had begun innocently enough on the Oguye. She had taken the first gruelling leg of the journey up to 'Fitzi-patriki' Lake by requisite steamer with its filthy decks, its

10

brazen rats. Disembarking at the French Mission, she had found to her delight a major Faung drama taking place.

Or perhaps it had been a great mission drama.

In any case there had been a stand-off between the French missionary, Louis Gilbert, who had brought his wife and two boys out to Africa with him, and the local Faung chief.

A pale and homesick Marie Gilbert had served Lily tea on the veranda of their bungalow. From this vantage point, Lily was able to watch while Marie had explained the particulars in a weary and long-suffering voice:

All the Faung women who sat under the great boya or 'meeting' tree were daubed with white paint on their faces and chests, and were chanting a low droning song. "They are mourning," explained Marie, "because the chief has become a Christian and Louis has told him that he may only have one wife. Now there are all his wives in mourning because he can only chose one, and without him, who are they, how can their brothers and uncles take them back, unmarriageable? And all the brothers and uncles are in a palaver because if the dowries are to be returned, what about reparations of a discarded wife which is a shameful thing? And who is to be kept, the first wife? By all rights it should be her. That's what Louis thinks. Except the second wife was given to the chief as part of a settlement in a dispute. If she is returned the dispute will be reopened. What about his favorite wife, number three who is about to bear a child who might be a son? It is possible that wife four is also with child, and wife five serves all the others and keeps his compound clean. The wives, you see, are sticking together in this when normally they bicker among each other endlessly."

"And what do you think?" Lily remembered asking, as she left the shade of Madame Gilbert's simple bungalow to investigate further.

Lilly couldn't hold back a snort of contempt when poor Marie had just shrugged helplessly and said, "What is there for me to think?"

The chief had looked utterly miserable on his sacred three-legged throne, shaded under a canopy of thatch. His

11

counselors sat about him on the bare ground and in the full sun, passing a gourd of beer, spitting to one side, then another. They spoke, each in turn while others chorused, "mm-mm-mm."

Louis Gilbert had been standing to one side, setting, resetting his pith helmet on his sweaty head. Fair hair with a complexion unsuited to the tropics, his face was flushed, blotchy. Or perhaps it had been his frustration. "I truly hoped for a resolution today," he had complained. "His soul is in grave danger."

"Why can't he be accepted as a Christian with all his wives?" Lily had asked.

He had given her a withering yet controlled look. "You must understand, Miss Bascombe, that is utterly impossible. As a Christian he may cleave to one wife only. There is no other course."

"But there is no provision for the discarded wives in their way of thinking. Can't you see that they are baffled. Everything has broken down. For the wives it is as though they are dead."

"They live in nothing but darkness." Louis held his temper but his words came out bitterly. Did Lily detect some pity in his tone? "Only their shadows are real to them. They live in terrible fear of that shadow world."

When Lily left for the Upper Oguye rapids by canoe some days later, the palaver was still in a deadlock, and she was glad to be away from the persistent mourning song which continued day and night, encouraged and supported by increasing numbers of relatives arriving from distant villages. A great wail was going up by more than fifty women, and the warriors were growing restless.

## 2.

Lily wrote in her journal: *From the start I wanted to explore the Upper Oguye by river canoe, proud of myself that I had already learned to keep my balance during my first few days at the French Mission. But how? Life groaned to a halt at the Mission, stagnant in the heat. A sense of doom and interminable waiting prevailed. I began to feel as contained as I had by my mother's bedside. I wanted to get on with my own business, and no one seemed interested in side-trips or adventures, so wrapped up were they in their spiritual affairs. And then, as luck would have it, I met Mbo.*

Their meeting had been as simple as it was unexpected. On the fourth day, when a party arrived from a village upriver to attend the great wailing, a young man left the canoes and sought her out. His bronze, muscular body was oiled and gleaming, enhanced by the copper bracelets on his upper and lower arms. He had obviously come down for a good time, and plenty of entertainment.

"Take you on river, Ma?" He queried, looking at her with dark eyes, so richly rimmed with lashes that she was reminded of the fringe of palms along the sea-side when she had taken her first steps on African soil.

Stunned, she looked him up and down. "English!"

"I learn from Mista Nohtoni." He saluted her crisply.

"Trader?" This Mr. Norton must have been an ex-military man, she thought—had he turned into a soldier of fortune?

"Mmm—mm." The shy warrior before her shook his head in assent.

"Where is he now?"

The young man shrugged.

"I would like to go for a picnic up the river." She said suddenly, decisively, hoping she had found a way onward. "Will you be my guide?"

"Pik' niki?"

"Yes, uh, a journey—to see, to look about. How do I say this—a feast for the spirit." She pointed in exasperation to her head and heart.

"Ah ah." He studied her, tilting his head. "You come to my village."

The arrangement had been as simple as that, the young man going off to find canoers willing to take her, while she brought out her trading-bags for a short expedition. Many of the youths were reluctant to leave the great stand-off going on between the chief and his wives. She watched him—how he went about his business. There was a dance about his walking, a humor in his face so that she felt in immediate kinship with him, an appreciation.

Perhaps the wailing had unnerved him too, because he made speedy preparations in the end, and they were underway. Only then did Lily find out he was also an expert canoer.

"But the rapids are treacherous!" Reverend Gilbert had been upset at her wanting to go upriver; he couldn't get it out of his mind that he was somehow responsible for her, but fortunately, he was too preoccupied by his impending spiritual conquest of the chief to be able to escort her himself.

How happy Lily had been to take to the river and escape, bored by Marie's habit of wringing her hands as she stood on the verandah. She was so unhappy and homesick that her mood began influencing Lily who couldn't seem to get away from it, even when taking to the forest paths on botanical explorations.

And Lily had been tired of Reverend Gilbert's arguments. Almost daily he would accost her with his closed mind. Earlier she had tried to debate with him but he could not understand why she was not affiliated with a mission. He had no humor. When she told him, 'I was called to Africa by Africa, not God,' she had to amend it quickly to: 'I was called to Africa by God to be a trader.' Perhaps she only redeemed herself in his eyes when she said that her purpose was to join Margery Poole wherever she had taken her mission, that she had to begin looking for her somewhere, and that she felt divine instruction to search further up the Oguye. It was after all, common knowledge that Margery Poole had taken her work into the interior somewhere, up one of the many rivers that drained into Fitzi-patriki.

Reluctantly, Reverend Gilbert had agreed to 'let her go alone.' Actually, he had looked relieved, waving a weary good-bye from the bank, his arm around Marie who waved too—a handkerchief in her hand. Until that moment, Lily had never believed that people actually waved handkerchiefs like that.

Mbo and his age-mate Peta had paddled her in the long dug-out canoe while two other youths, Masa and Topi paddled her supplies, singing with every stroke.

Mbo had a very small knowledge of English; Lily had a very small knowledge of Faung, and so they began to teach each other with signs. She began to understand the songs that moved them from one place to another throughout the day. The meaning of their song that day was simple, *up the Oguye, up the Oguye,* but the intent was more complicated. They were appealing to the river spirit; they were going against the current, and so, even in this contradiction, sought to find an easy channel. If they were correct in their purpose, they would find their way. And she would find hers.

She had not found Miss P. on her month long excursion up the Oguye; she had found the Faung people, those away from the sphere of the French Mission. They became her family as she had never had it with her invalid mother, not her distant, mostly absent father, nor her cold, reserved relatives, least of all her arrogant, aloof brother.

In particular she had found the Faung women. It was not an easy thing at first, because the men were the ones who came forward to trade, barter and debate. Fitzi-patriki had certainly not written much about them.

Maybe she would have had to remain within that male domain, if she had wanted to trade tobacco for fetishes. But

15

part of her trading was to discover plant specimens, and this led her with her trading beads to the women. It turned out that they were the experts at gathering plants. She went with them into the forest, moving with ease far below the canopy of the gigantic trees, wanting in particular, something special to take back to Marie for her garden. Perhaps a flowering vine would cheer her up.

Lily's main guide was the witch doctor's co-wife. She was old by their standards, perhaps five years Lily's senior—at thirty-five her body had a good ten to fifteen years more in physical aging. She was not emaciated but shrunken, her breasts withered, her stomach laced with stretch marks, her face creased. Her filed teeth were white when she broke into her smile with her wide lips, and her eyes, shadowed, even hooded one moment, would twinkle when she was pleased.

She had brightened at the the sound of Lily's name, cackling hoarsely because it sounded oddly like her own 'Llile, a name beginning with a deep, throaty sound 'uh,' but so united with the flowing 'l' as to be indistinguishable where one began and the other ended. A new sound. She asked what Lily's name meant—all this inquiry took a long time to understand, but finally Lily conveyed 'flower' by finding the closest thing to a lily she could; this also took a long time. In turn 'Llile explained her name by mixing certain leaves together, very carefully chosen leaves. She handed them to Lily as she gathered them, naming each and Lily wrote down a phonetic version of the words in her book, as well as the shape of the leaf. Then she mixed them using a mortar to crush them. The paste she made, she held up to Lily's face on the tips of her dark fingers to smell and taste.

She had pointed with satisfaction to the paste, then pointed to her womb. Lily thought to understand—that the mixture was her name, that it had to do with childbearing or strengthening oneself for childbearing, But it took many days to really understand that her name was the actual act of mixing the right ingredients, that her name meant the very act of sorcery. Yes, it was also linked to the core of womanhood, the source of power.

And Lily meant but a flower? Lily wanted it to mean much

more. Now, at least she understood some of the laughter she had caused when she introduced herself. Lily, a sorceress?

More importantly, through 'Llile, she had been taken to a place she had not seen in the village before. Yes, she was familiar with the open arena where the men came to meet; knew the arrangements of huts according to marriage and positions of each wife; could pick out the huts where the older children stayed separated by gender. Now she was taken to a hidden place within the village, a place protected by taboo. They walked down a path which had small clearings in the tangle of bush, to one side, then the other. Each clearing was a place of offering with statues of various ancestral spirits. A typical offering was a small gourd full of food, bundles of items wrapped in bark or leaves. Many of the statues were female and stained with what Lily took to be resin and later found out was actually blood discharged during menses.

Crawling through a low opening in a thick fence made of thorn branches, first announcing themselves in song, they were answered by a chorus of women. After passing through this wall they went through yet another made of wattle and daubed mud. At last they were in a compound consisting of two huts and a tidy courtyard; no half-wild fowl running around here, no weaned children.

Diligently, Lily took all this in but only after a long while did it dawn on her that the youngest girls were those who had already passed through puberty rights. Many women sat in the sunny courtyard oiling each other's skin or hair, hands rippling over each others naked bodies so that Lily found that she had stopped and stared. Others prepared yams over the fire or else were engrossed with elaborate bead or mat work. She could hear the low tones of women within the darkness of the huts; resting, she calculated, writing her observations down for later reference. *Even the lowliest of wives*, she noted, *seem to have respite here from the constant pecking order. If only it were so in the village.*

'Llile then had taken her down yet another path where they came upon a rushing stream which cascaded over rocks, filled brimming pools. Some women were bathing their babies. She indicated that this was a good place to bathe.

Lily was overjoyed, observing the other women discreetly as she could—two young women in particular who sat in the tumbling water between two rocks, caressing each other, one sitting between the others legs, head back, while the other fondled her breasts, their words to each other lost in the tumult of rushing water.

Flushing, Lily had turned away. It reminded her of something long ago when she was a child—sitting in the lap of a woman once who whispered to her. A woman—not her mother—a woman who had been the first to mention Africa to her. Perhaps it was the nakedness of the women now that made her blush in an odd confusion. Or was it simply the way one held the other? Lily turned away to dabble her own hands in the water, feel it push between her fingers in its hurry.

This river, the Upper Oguye, thrilled her in every way—less mosquitoes and no crocodiles—unlike the wide river entering Lake Fitzi-patriki where keeping one's balance in a canoe meant holding onto one's life as well. But to actually submerse herself in water!—was it possible? Not since a tin tub down on the coast had she had such a chance.

But Lily had been terribly shy over her own nakedness, confessing to her journal later that she had waited until dark under a waxing but not yet full moon. The women were not interested in bathing at night but were gathered by a large fire in the compound. And so she made her way with secret delight, stripped her clothes off in an act of great daring and abandon, lowered herself gently into one of the frothy pools; listened to the eerie calls of tree frogs. The smooth rocks cradled her like one woman had cradled the other, and the swirling water caressed her skin. Stimulated, overjoyed, touched in the very real sense of the word—she felt loved. And stayed for a long time.

Among these Faung women she had felt recognized, not seen as some strange, colorless creature wearing odd and encumbering fetishes; not seen as some member of a remote tribe which the Faung thought came like fish from the great water (which was how they saw the English ships,) but seen at last, as a woman to be welcomed and taken in by her own kind.

When Lily had taken her leave, after one full month, to check back at the mission station, 'Llile had given her a pouch on a thong necklace; tied it securely and deliberately around her neck amid a lengthy and animated speech punctuated with explosive clicks that she made first with her tongue, then with her lips; cackling in conclusion.

Urgently, Lily nudged Mbo who stood beside her. "Tell me what she is saying."

"How do you do?" he answered compliantly, grinning and translating nothing for her benefit. "Tea time, Ma. We go now."

Exasperated, Lily had had to make up her own interpretation, hoping it meant good fortune, a safe journey, and success in finding—as she logged in her diary—Miss P.

Lily had returned to the mission from her trading upriver with great anticipation as to how the matter of the chief's faith had been resolved. When she arrived back, stepping out of the canoe, she was relieved to see the open ceremonial arena empty. The chief's stool was gone but not the thatched canopy. The shade beneath the great, sacred boya tree held three children playing in the dirt. She went to stand in the shade out of reverence, gazing up into the great, gnarled branches; remembering the dismal, unnerving wail.

The Gilbert bungalow itself had seemed strangely empty. The Gilbert boys who usually paraded up and down the verandah trying to keep their embroidered shirts clean, were nowhere in sight.

Setting her things aside for the moment and with questions on the tip of her tongue, she was met by the Gilbert's 'house boy.' "What has happened?" she demanded, sensing that whatever it was, it wasn't good.

The Faung youth who had given up his loin cloth for shorts, shrugged impassively and pointed to a neat grave, signs of wilted flowers beneath the wooden cross. At first she was sure that some skirmish had broken out, that Louis had met with a bloody death. The answer was much simpler. The ancestors had not been pleased and surely someone had set a witch-doctor upon poor Louis Gilbert. Alas, he had come down with a fever, crying out in delirium for five days, dying on the sixth. Only then had the women stopped their wailing, taking up a different chant for the dead. And the chief had gone home to his wives.

Then what of Marie and the boys? Gone, gone on the steamer down river only yesterday. Yesterday? She knew that could mean days ago.

At first she was anxious because she had left the bulk of her goods in care of the Gilberts, and she saw that the outer warehouse, always kept under lock and key, had been smashed into. But her belongings, all her packs which she had left in her room, were untouched.

Lily took some roots she had brought back with her for Marie, and went to plant them at the corner of the verandah. Someday a vine would be climbing there, the orange flowers blooming after the rains. She didn't think that the witch-doctor had anything to do with Louis' death. Surely no witch-doctor could be a match for the power of fifty angry, wailing women. She couldn't help but wonder at the miserable will of the fifty-first woman also—Marie.

The emptiness under the boya tree, the echo in the mud-daubed bungalow was eerie and unsettling. The open, thatched church stood abandoned. Mbo approached her and said it was not a good place to stay, that he and the others would go to the village nearby.

But she had stayed. Why? She did not rightly know. Was it because she needed something to cling to in her indecision about the next step? It was obvious she had to move on— soon, tomorrow; it could be months before someone was sent out to start up the mission again. She didn't envy that person's task. By the time they came, they would find the forest already taking over. If they came after the rainy season, they would find rotten thatch, termite eaten beams. And always, always the fever. Sitting on the verandah in the night with a hurricane lamp for light and comfort, she shivered, writing everything down in her journal. No wonder Marie Gilbert had fled—she who had not known the comfort and happiness of a Faung women's compound....

Ah, but there had been much more to that story, much

more to the fifty wailing women. Things she knew she didn't know. Of course she would tell Miss P—ask for her opinion.

She looked around in the vast African morning as the lion roared. This was her loneliness: That she wanted to tell someone what she knew about this Africa that was so different and exciting from anything she had ever known before. And she held the anticipation that surely, Miss Poole would understand. She thumbed through her field notes, still dry and clean from the arduous ride on top of her head the day before in the swamp, adding new thoughts in the margins so that she wouldn't forget anything. For the time being the pen and page would have to be her only confidant.

# 3.

Now, ever pressing on towards the Robolo, Lily's party left behind the rocky banks, the expanse of swamp and made their way through the lush undergrowth of the dense forest, climbing the escarpment to the plain above. Mbo had promised a spring of clear, bubbly water which they found in the first hour, gushing up among the gigantic ferns.

Ecstatic, Lily took the time to drink deeply and wash up as much as her lack of privacy allowed. And while she was aware of her Victorian etiquette, she could not bring herself to even wash her hair as much as she wanted to. It was not the time or place.

Her companions filled their gourds and animal stomaches with water while she filled up her trusty goat-skin bag— brought home to England by her father from Greece after one of his excursions, and which she had claimed from his amassed souvenirs. Slinging it over her shoulder she found great comfort in its weight against her hip.

They proceeded up game trails, Mbo checking spoor along the way. He made comments down the line to his peers. She was used to that—the conversation of interested hunters who are consistently wary and inquisitive even when on other business.

A tumult in the tree tops from a flock of angry birds cautioned them about a snake. Mbo craned his neck to see where it was, then pointed it out to Lily. Thick,as a vine it lay motionless along a branch fifty feet above them, intent on robbing eggs, no doubt. Lily rested her hand on the pistol stuck in her sash, but she was a disinterested hunter, and the party made their way again.

They walked single file in their habitual order, Mbo first, followed by Peta, the stalwart first mate, behind him Ngobi, The Ugly One. Lily didn't think of him particularly ugly; he wasn't as lithe physically perhaps, but his face was pleasant enough. His name came from his disposition when he drank. After him came Masa with the talking-drum, Lily at some distance behind with Topi bringing up the rear, according to his special training.

There was a rhythm to their order, to their pace as they began their day together. Since starting off, they had gone by river canoe as far as possible up a tributary, then cut through the forest, next across the infamous swamp to continue towards another major river. Since Lily had worked herself all the way up the Oguye River with no sign of Miss P, she was set on exploring the next river, intent on working her way down it.

And it was now, as they left the Oguye region, that her Faung companions became more wary, uncertain. She knew some of the tribes they were to meet up with had truces with them, made marriage exchanges, also traded—in particular, the bamboo and black clay, rich in that region; they were for the most part, 'distant relatives.' Still, any tribe was fair game to be raided for women, and any women who were captured were treated shabbily. For Lily, it was her first encounter with real slavery, and while each tribe saw itself as superior, counter-raids were not uncommon. Meeting up with other people could also mean the possibility of hostile skirmishes. She hoped that her own party's motivation was different, knowing that Peta's keen interest in bamboo spears over Robolo way, had helped her succeed in mounting her expedition. The one difference was that no one from their village had ever taken such a northerly route before; they couldn't be sure what they'd meet up with. She knew that they sought safe passage with her as an excuse—a trader bent on meeting up with Nelson and Brodwick Ltd. down the Robolo at the Trading Station. Admittedly, she had the dull hope that her oddity as a single, white woman was not an obstacle, if the people she met up with had any contact with Miss P.

Absorbed by her concerns, she walked with her head bent, contemplating the various tracks in the earth besides those of her party—weren't those some kind of cat print? Is that what Mbo was remarking about?—when a burst of alarm, some blast of fury erupted ahead of her, bringing her up short. Masa was on the ground in front of her, a massive swatch of black spots and claws flattening him, great white fangs gripping his throat. Frozen where she was, Lily's hand acted for her; it whipped out her pistol and fired at the great cat head, right between the eyes, fired into its audacious, predatory triumph, shattering its brain.

The shot resounded throughout the forest, a blasphemy shaking the trees to their roots while awakening an outrage of animal cries, particularly the shrieks of monkeys.

The leopard jerked with the force of the wound, then lay bleeding on top of Masa. There was a jerking of muscle as it died. Then its claws retracted slowly as the muscles gave in, the fangs released, the fire ebbed away and the once beautiful head with its gaping hole, lolled to the side

"Ho," Mbo exclaimed, leaning over Masa, and pointing to the bullet hole. A spear bristled in the leopard's neck. She had not been the only one to act quickly, before the bullet struck, Peta had found his chance to spear the leopard without damaging Masa.

But for Masa it was too late. The leopard had pierced his throat; the blood spurted from him like a butchered animal. The life left his eyes, while all around him, the rest of the party hovered in shock and helplessness.

The echo of the shot still rang in Lily's ears. Her arm ached from the kick-back. She shook with the understanding of what she had done, or even that the bullet had found its mark. She had never really shot anything before, and it made her sick. Or was her head reeling to see Masa sprawled out on the path like that, the leopard's paw still retreating across his chest?

Why did everyone just stand there, stupefied? They looked at her with astonishment, their noses twitching as they sniffed the odd, sulphurous gun smoke, while what she noticed was the rank smell of cat hide, and the metallic stench of blood. Then she wondered—had they never witnessed such a thing before. Had Mbo's trader, Mr. Norton never fired a shot? It seemed unlikely.

"Get the leopard off of him," she barked, her voice shrill with tension. Topi dropped his bundle and went to pull the cat away. Masa was indeed dead. Lily could feel no pulse in his arm.

Mbo who usually acted quickly to see to matters, simply stood there, clucking in his throat. Then he knelt down and carefully removed the fetish of protection from Masa's neck. The leather thong was broken by the leopard's teeth. He held the broken necklace up as though he were holding a dead snake, his expression full of disdain. He spat in resigned disgust and the other's took up a refrain—quick comments going back and forth, punctuated with clicks of the tongue and cheek, hums in the throat.

She remembered that she was the foreigner, and though she ordained where their trek went, she had no say in matters like this. She could imagine Fitzi-patriki ordering his men to skin the leopard, bury the body with no thought to their surly responses.

She bent down to inspect the leopard which had so suddenly leapt out of nowhere. Then she remembered how she had become aware of its presence, or of its tracks at any rate, only moments before it sprang. She shuddered; with her head bent for close inspection of the path, why hadn't the leopard jumped on her? It would have been a quick death. How much had Masa known? As hunters, wouldn't they have been keenly aware? Why, Mbo was always bragging how he could smell things out, constantly proving it to her by bringing back the exact quarry within minutes.

Vividly, she recalled that they had all been walking normally, no sudden stealth or shift to their stride. Her hands ran over the fur, still warm, felt the tough muscle beneath the hide. The leopard was a female, small, no signs of teats. She sighed with relief that she hadn't orphaned any cubs. Small consolation. Gazing above her she saw where the leopard must have crouched some ten feet above.

"You didn't see her?" She addressed Mbo, realizing that

she blamed him. He simply shrugged, returned in English, "She was no there, Ma."

His response put her off. She suspected that he only spoke English when he was in a flippant mood—his form of 'fever humor,' or when he was absorbed in something he didn't want to take the time to explain. She felt put in her place, shut out, and she didn't like it.

She wanted explanations. She wanted the whole episode erased from her memory. She wanted them to do it all over again, this time with Mbo sounding a warning, halting the procession and Masa still alive.

If Mbo had not seen the leopard, where had it been when he passed under the tree? Had it been there all the time but his eyes elsewhere? And why hadn't Peta or Ngobi seen it? Three people! Three people, each about ten paces behind the other. Was it simply that the leopard, having seen the first, made ready, but was not in position until Masa came?

"What do we do with the body?" she demanded of Mbo.

He was rubbing the fetish with a leaf, matter of factly at that, while he continued his low conversation. Ngobi cut one of the leopard's ears and gave it to her to put in her own pouch, and the other he gave to Mbo who stuck it in Masa's small leather one. Lily knew that items significant to Masa were contained there and meant to protect him. He had been deeply failed. Peta handed Mbo some more leaves in which they wrapped the necklace before Mbo stowed it in the pouch he wore round his own neck. Although his motions were simple, they seemed to have deep significance. None of the men seemed at all interested in the bloody body at their feet, but they grunted in satisfaction after Mbo had put away the necklace.

"We must take his strength back to the place of his ancestors," Mbo explained at last in Faung, as though she were an acceptable member of the party again. He used the same word that meant power and also, breath. It was a word that defied definition in her own language, a word that meant spirit, the very essence of life that flowed through everything.

That very 'power' had flowed through the leopard also. In a clash like a jolt of lightning, they had broken the flow. No,

26

Lily corrected herself—she had helped to break it. The leopard was about to take Masa into herself and so the power would have continued but the gunshot had interrupted that flow.

The men lifted Masa's body and hurled it from the path into the dense undergrowth. With quick, sharp strokes of their scythes, they skinned the leopard, rubbing the inner side with dirt, Mbo hanging it from his shoulders down his back. Then they portioned out Masa's bundle.

Mbo handed her the drum. "You carry this, Ma. Who will be our drum?" His tone was that flippant one again, a grin spreading across his face.

She smiled reluctantly, taking it. "Doesn't anyone else know how?"

He brought all the fingers of his right hand together, the way he would when he ate, and tapped his chest, "No have..."

"...what it takes," she finished for him.

Lily understood with the loss of Masa whole balance of the expedition changed, and the men were in the throes of spiritual confusion which they still had to correct.

"I refuse to take it as an omen," she muttered under her breath, fingering the hide bands along the sides of the drum, examining the taut skins on either end. Tucking the mute instrument under her arm as she had seen Masa do, she picked up her portmanteau with her other hand. Chin up, she ordered herself, and then aloud, "Let us proceed then."

Shortly, they began their ascent of the escarpment. The first sign was more sunlight and a rockier path, the rocks growing larger until they were like haphazard steps with great tree roots tangled among them. Lily loved the shapes of the coarse boulders, their fissures full of red lichens. They seemed to vibrate with an energy as though they had absorbed the early morning roar of the lion, as though they rang with the shot from her revolver, even as they soaked up heat from the sun.

Once they were above the forest she was drenched with sweat, and she couldn't get rid of the smell of blood in her nose and throat. Meanwhile, what her companions sang about was not the loss of Masa, a life, but the fact that they were coming into 'enemy' territory without a drum—a mouth.

Lily's lingering anger was that no one seemed to accept responsibility for the misadventure, not even any shame at having missed out on the clues of the leopard's presence. It was as though what had happened had to do with Masa's relationship with greater forces, that whatever was out of balance with the excursion was because of his flaws or something he had done or not done. Or perhaps they thought someone had brought it upon him, sent the leopard there. She didn't know his history.

Meanwhile they had no drummer. From what they were singing, they seemed to think his message would have brought them nothing but trouble, a kind of 'good riddance to bad rubbish' song.

In contrast Lily felt sentimental, very European. Masa had been the one who taught her how to paddle a canoe. She remembered that he had shown her how to hit crocodiles on their snouts if any came too close, an aggressive action to 'speak' to the croc: I am not for you and you are not for me. It was something that especially the children sang when they rode in canoes.

She could only think of Masa in glowing terms. She had hired him to teach her canoeing after Mbo had left her stranded two days longer than agreed, what with his own business up some river. And she had traded away all she had brought, having to resort to bartering with her supply of shirts until she had only one left. Wanting independence from then on, or at least the opportunity for escape, she made sure she could maneuver herself anywhere she needed by canoe, whacking crocodile snouts for all she was worth.

Again and again she reminded herself that there had been no reason for the leopard to spring at that moment. It had simply happened. But she couldn't shake the incident off while trudging steadily upwards between and over rocks, grabbing for gnarled roots as she went. She wanted to understand how her companions felt, yet could not get past her own feelings.

Strangely enough, the climb invigorated her as though in

her rage, she were gathering great strength. Maybe it was all the iron in the rocks about her, evident, due to the blackened wrecks of trees thrust here and there— ideal lightning rods. Yes, she could feel the rocks bristling with power, a low tremble in her body.

Put that in your map, Mr. Fitzi-patriki: the land of the Talking Rocks, she thought tersely.

"Do you feel it?" She addressed Mbo who had stopped, waiting. "The strength in the rocks?" The breath, the power, the life. It was the same word.

He shook his head, consenting, "Mm-mm-mm," as though she were stating the obvious like 'the sun is hot.' How he does indulge me, she thought.

By way of reply, he pointed with his spear upwards to a ledge full of baboons. It was as though he had conjured them, because the rocks came alive with their grey-brown forms, fierce snouts and beady eyes. Only a moment ago she had seen nothing. Almost as soon as Mbo pointed them out, a large male began barking as it leapt down to a ledge closer. His call of alarm was answered until there was an echoing racket up and down the rocks from all directions, much leaping and agitation as the troop edged away, the dominant males jumping closer again, then retreating.

Lily might have taken it in stride but since the leopard attack she felt edgy, threatened.

Mbo stopped, waited, the group silent behind him. His stance was relaxed but she knew he was poised with his spear. She could see the tendons in his hands flexing. He looked with noble disdain upon the aggressive baboon, a look beyond anything she had seen him give crocodiles. Before she had time to consult with him, he leapt from one rock to another, brandishing his spear and hurling insults at the baboons, "You are dogs; no, you are worse. Even the hyena is better than you!"

Peta, Ngobi and Topi followed his example, coughing in imitation of the baboon bark, but full of mockery.

The male baboons stood stock still. The leader jumped up and down barking as the others retreated, their eyes still staring hostilely. They all moved along, staying carefully just out of reach.

29

This uneasy stand-off remained for the rest of the climb, baboons jumping back and forth along the ledges at parallels. Lily's hand stayed on her pistol but she didn't brandish it. Fitzi patriki had written about baboons, that they were like dogs. He had never had any qualms about shooting them like so many decoys at a country fair. This was the first time she had seen them, the fear and excitement rising in her throat. They were not creatures of the forest but of the open grassland like the lion.

She couldn't wait to see the new terrain.

The sun was sinking though storm clouds in the west as they reached the plateau. All the land was bathed in an orange glow, and for the first time, Lily could turn and see the wide magnificent view of the swamp far below. It stretched out, a flat, charred smudge, but from her new vantage point she could see the forest way in the distance, and also how the swamp narrowed towards the west, becoming greener. They had been five to ten miles off their mark. She debated whether she was looking at a clogged and dying river, or else the source of one very much alive further on.

While the rest of her party set up camp, Peta and Ngobi going off after game, she sat on a rock, sketching the view and adding to her map. If the expanse below her had been one of clear water, it would have been a wide lake. As it was, she could see that there were plenty of water fowl reeling about in the coming twilight, and so she put it down as simply, Black Lake, with no intention of ever recommending it as a route. Her view also told her that Black Lake was a low point in the landscape, a giant sieve.

And as she sat, the sun disappearing, she felt that longing again, a loneliness in the vast magnificence around her. That she had traversed the swamp, climbed to her present look-out, seemed insignificant. A timelessness defied her.

It was not that she felt home-sick. Certainly not. The clog of people in London, her dismal family house, tiresome social teas among relatives she thought dull—all were things she had no desire to go back to. More to the point, there was no one to go back to, as much as she wanted to tell her world of what she saw. She could hardly think of her brother as someone to pour out this passion to, for all the time she spent with him, infrequent and cold as it was. Perhaps now that she was gone for awhile he'd find someone to marry, therefore sparing her the duty of managing his life. That her thoughts turned to her brother made her even more lonely.

Passing her mood off as fatigue, the end of the day, she called to Mbo gently, asking if the water was hot for tea yet. Shortly, with a hot tin mug between her hands, she sat near the smoky fire to avoid the mosquitoes.

Their camp was in a grassy open area, bordered by rocks and scrubby trees. She could hear Mbo cutting long grass, his scythe swishing. He was building a thatched canopy for her; already Topi was lashing some poles together, one place for her and the bundles, another for the men. She understood by their actions that they were expecting rain.

She slept that night, propped against her baggage, waking up to the sky shaking. Just my luck to camp out next to a magnetic field, she grumbled mostly because she was deeply impressed. Why did she have the feeling that they had chosen the very spot that drew the storms? Heavy rain exploded, testing the hastily thatched roof of her make-shift hut which held, except for steady trickles here and there. With some maneuvering those places could be avoided; water splashing from the low eaves and off the ground in sheets was unavoidable. The night was a matter of being grateful for small comforts. At least the mosquitoes were held at bay.

Shivering at daybreak, puddles around her glistening, Lily was ready to hike. Her damp clothes made her irritable. And more than anything she wanted to bathe. Perhaps they would find a village today, and if she were lucky she might be given a hut of her own to stay in. Besides, she was ready for the reassuring company of women with their own kind of musical conversation. Maybe she needed that even more that a chance to bathe. Why did she have the feeling that she would still be wearing swamp mud on her by the time they reached the Robolo which could still be days away?

Was it too strange for her to picture the Gilbert's simple bungalow with enamel pitcher and basin? Or even the damp, mold encrusted houses on the colonial coast with tin or cracked, porcelain tubs and tepid water. These trappings of civilization were nothing compared to how she missed particular rock-pools with their bubbling waters. Her only cure seemed to be to shoulder her load and trudge on, hoping to be distracted by things either beautiful or remarkable at any rate. Since yesterday she had acquired a new sense of foreboding; not everything was simple adventure. She suspected every turn, every looming hour.

She could not get the image of Masa and the leopard out of her mind.

And she hadn't really been able to shake what had happened back at French Mission. Louis Gilbert had died and been buried on the same day. There were Faung tribesmen very familiar with White customs around death, and willing to dig their graves. She didn't wonder that his grave was being dug as he tossed in unsuspecting delirium within the bungalow; from what she had seen at the coast such preparations were normal. The grave diggers were so eager there that they had advance graves dug and covered with tidy wooden lids.

It wasn't hard for her to imagine poor Marie pacing the verandah in vexation while the many women wailed under the boya tree. What amulet would Marie take back to Louis' ancestors? His pipe perhaps. His Bible.

He, like Masa, was a discarded body far from home.

Was it morbid of her to wonder what Mbo would have been faced with had the leopard decided to spring on her instead of Masa? She decided she had best keep herself hale and hearty rather than subject her Faung companions to the problem of what to do with a dead white women in the middle of her expedition.

One thing cheered her up considerably, and that was the certainty of her alliance with the Upper Oguye Faung women. She missed them. If I have to get the fever anywhere, let it be back among them, she prayed. Let me just get back to them. And it was as though they had an answer for her, because as she and her party set into a fast pace through tall grass, past rocky outcroppings, they came upon a woman.

# 4.

Lily Bascombe told herself that to pray daily for the successful discovery of Miss Margery Poole's whereabouts was only right and proper, knowing full well she was asking for too much. It was like wanting water, knowing she didn't have enough and that the terrain would only get drier. She regretted that she had not asked for a female companion in the party—one of the Faung women she had left behind. It hadn't occurred to her then to ask one of them to come along. For one thing, none of her porters were yet married, and the ultimate wages they would receive from Lily meant dowry when they got home.

Now Lily was keenly aware that some sort of prayer had been answered, even if not the one she had consciously intended, because they came upon a Faung woman.

She had a wattle-and-thatch hut near a stand of trees. Not much of a hut, but more substantial that the lean-to Lily had had the night before.

A young woman with her bronze skin, short hair strung with beads, wearing a beaded 'skirt' across her pelvis, she stood like a statue in the path ahead of them. She held a baby slung in antelope skin on her hip. By the colored strands she wore, made from dyed seeds, Lily understood her to be married: brown for a menstruating woman, green for the fertility she would bring in marriage both to the land of her husband, and in terms of the children she would bear him. She did not have the distinctive 'v' pattern in yellow that a co-wife would display in her beading, nor did she have the bluish-black of a hefty dowry which was more common than not.

33

As soon as the woman saw them she sat down, her legs straight out in front of her and her baby swung around to sit on her thighs. This was a position of deference in the presence of other tribal members, either among other wives, or with any elders, and, certainly,with men. By this very passive posture she took, she was also indicating relief at seeing some of her own people.

Mbo called to the woman, a standard if not surprised greeting. Lily and her party stopped and put their bundles down. Lily realized that for a woman to be on her own in such an unlikely place was not customary.

While Mbo spoke to her, Lily took a few steps towards the hut, bending slightly and without any thought to being nosy, stuck her head in the doorway. A woven grass mat on the ground, a small fire circle and a gourd were things that didn't speak of permanence. No clay pots, no skins, no mortar and pestle.

She turned back to stand with the men, towering over the young woman who averted her eyes. Lily had the sense to squat and all except Mbo did the same, Topi passing a stomach of water around.

Lily tried to follow the conversation with its proscribed punctuations on both sides, its guttural clicks and hums— faces stoically inexpressive all the while.

Finally, peeved at her lack of comprehension, she snapped, "Translate!"

Mbo held up the palm of his hand to stay her, then dropped his arm and turned to her. "She is sent out from her village. This is very bad. She say that the other wives say she poisoned the husband. But she say she did not. They are jealous because he favored her. She say he die of a witch-doctor's curse by his co-wife. She is blamed instead and sent out from the village to die."

"Good gracious," Lily stood up feeling offended. Was it just her English sense of justice? Certainly it offended her deep sense of loyalty to her gender. "Do you know her family?"

He put up his hand again, his head nodding sharply as he spoke once more to the woman. Her baby, a toddler, had begun to nurse, but every so often turned his head with round, dark eyes to stare at Lily. There was more curiosity than fear in his gaze, while his mother spoke in a wail, holding her head in her hands the way the Faung do when they are being chastised.

Mbo explained further, "She say she is on her way to her mother's home but comes to the swamp and is stop because of the child. So she come back here where she has rested before. She roots here or traps small game, and there is water not far. Sometimes she must spend the night in the tree because of the lions. She say she is waiting for the dry season so she can find a way across the swamp."

"Will it dry up?" Lily was astonished that over five feet of swamp water and mud might dry up enough to walk across.

He shrugged. "This is what she say to me. She is trying to get back home but she knows this is no good. Her uncle of her mother cannot get the dowry back. She is in disgrace. She has been cursed."

"And she has been living here? How long?"

While the other men passed the water gourd back and forth to each other, Ngobi lighting up the pipe, each of them adding unhelpful 'mm-mms' at random, Mbo said, "She has been here during the rains. She does not know where she is." He looked about restlessly. "We must not stay in this place."

"What on earth do you mean?"

"She is sent out. Away."

"Well, there's no question but that she must come with us." Lily announced in no uncertain terms. "She's a Faung!"

Mbo wore his face of patience as he always did when Lily refused to understand the custom.

Lily blustered, refusing to acknowledge his reluctance, "If she no longer has a husband or a dowry, then I shall take her on as my personal ward. I will convey her back to her family with appropriate payment or else arrange a fitting marriage. I certainly can't just leave her here. It's as good as death."

"But she is cursed, Ma."

"Not by us! By finding her on our route, we have lifted the curse! After all, you are carrying Masa back with you after he died in a strange place, and wasn't he cursed?"

Mbo looked at her with his own brand of skepticism—his thick upper lip catching on his neatly filed teeth. A gesture, that would make the likes of Fitzi-patriki swear to the existence of cannibalism in the rain forest.

She laughed and clapped her hands so that the baby jumped in his mother's lap. "What is her name, and the name of her baby?"

Mbo turned the question to the woman.

"Shi w'zi, mm, Mtoli."

"Shiwezi? I know what that means: 'by the river.' Tell Shiwezi to bring her belongings. Explain that I have a dowry for her and that she must come with me, that I will take care of her."

Mbo explained, then turned to Lily, amusement in his eyes. "She wants to know if you are a co-wife, where is your husband, and what wife is she?"

"Tell her my husband is far down Shi Robolo and that I am on business for him, that actually I am looking for another white wife, but she'll do."

He took her joke in stride; it was perhaps the first joke she had told that would amuse the Faung, evident by the throaty laughter from the other porters.

Lily hoped that neither Mr. Nelson, nor Mr. Brodwick of the Trading Company would mind this impromptu marriage to one of them she had just performed by proxy. But the arrangement seemed to suit Shiwezi because she rose slowly to meet her new fate, and went to retrieve the few items in the hut.

"By the way, ask her if she has seen any other woman like me, a white woman?" Lily threw out with faint hope.

Shortly, Mbo returned a respectfully doleful answer, "No, Ma. She does not know of such a woman."

A few moments later the young bronze woman, muscular and graceful in her listless way, stood ready, her face unreadable, her child tied to her back and her possessions on top of her head.

Then all except Mbo, picked up their bundles.

As if getting the last word in, or else indicating his superior role in the expedition, Mbo had clearly left his bundle for Shiwezi to carry. He was already striding on ahead to scout out the way. Lily watched in horror as Shiwezi added the bundle to what she already carried—without question, not even surprise.

"She can carry very much, very much!" Peta said quickly, as if excusing his age-mate. "She can carry much more than any man on her head. Woman is good for this."

"I'll say," Lily muttered angrily, gripping the handle of her portmanteau. "She has obviously never been considered worth much to anyone, except perhaps to do the cleaning up and play the role of scape-goat. I understand her position clearly. By God, I will make certain she is wearing blue beads by the time she leaves me."

The expedition got underway again—four men and two women. It made the leopard attack on Masa all the more auspicious in Lily's mind—that his blatant absense should be righted by the presence of a woman, all in balance again. But the order of things was different this time. Shiwezi as 'second' wife, walked behind—a valuable wife for all that, since she had already proven she could bear a son.

And Lily, the 'co-wife,' felt considerably more cheerful than she had in quite awhile. It was as though she dared breathe the hot African air again and not suffocate, as though she could take in the sights and sounds with renewed interest. She actually felt like humming along to the song the men had started.

The grassland seemed to team with life, tortoises across the path—a few snakes too, plenty of alarmed bushpigs and antelope, and as always, the many kinds of birds: hawks wheeling high in the sky, egrets and maribou storks in and about the trees. The group stopped long enough at an ochre, weedy waterhole to make certain no lion lolled about, before taking their own mid-day rest.

There, Shiwezi began to tend to basic camp chores, especially the cooking, instead of Mbo who took off hunting, dutifully leaving Ngobi to keep watch. With her trusty tin cup of tea beside her, Lily lay back on one of the packs in a patch of shade, staring into the sky through gnarled branches, while watching Shiwezi out of the corner of her eye.

With the woven grass mat, Shiwezi always had a seat, a place. There, where she unrolled it, she sat and nursed Mtoli or dandled him on her outstretched arms so that his legs kicked as he jumped up and down, gurgling with laughter. Lily liked the musical notes of his mother's laugh in return. All was well with the world.

It was at this moment that she realized with her sense of etiquette that with another woman present, at last, she could wash her hair without feeling vulnerable. She realized how pleased she was to have come across Shiwezi, how important it was to have another woman along.

Making her way down to the water hole with a calabash, she finally let down her hair. As she dipped the gourd into the water just enough to let the clear liquid seep over the edge into the bowl, so minimizing the amount of weedy particles in her rinse, she saw the depth of the sky reflected. A shiver ran through her, a thrill of connection with something; she didn't quite know what in particular. Was it the water itself, mysteriously cloaked or clogged with green, even as the obsidian lake behind her had been choked? In the dazzling sunlight, there was a shadow to it all, a secret whispered, words she couldn't quite hear or didn't quite know. But it left her trembling with joy.

She sat at the water's edge unable to move, the sweat trickling down her forehead. Undoing the knot of hair on the back of her head, she let her dark strands fall over her face. Bending forward, she lifted the calabash, poured, the cool water washing over her scalp. Again, again she dipped ever so slowly, watching as the water welled up in the bowl, filling with sky again, the sparkle of the sun. Pouring it over her, it dripped off like laughter. Laughing like baby Mtoli did.

Lathering her head with soap, she thought, I shall get myself a grass mat too, and then I shall always have a place. How simple. Squeezing her eyes shut as she washed the soap away, she could see Shiwezi in her mind's eye, and felt envious. A young woman cursed once yes, but not any longer. A young woman with a beaded band around her waist, her shiny skin otherwise open to the sun. And if I cast my clothes aside, Lily thought sourly, I am nothing but shamefully naked. Her breasts were, after all, hidden things she bared only in the dark, and even then did not look at.

Why did she want to hurl all her belongings into the pool, everything, even her portmanteau, hurl it all into the depths to sink beneath the weedy surface? It was as though some voice taunted her, someone behind her, someone just beyond the edge of her vision, telling her that she too, could cast aside her shoes and walk on the thick soles of her feet over the game trails with nothing more than a rolled up mat of grass on her head, a calabash in her hand, and perhaps a baby, rocking with every step, on her back.

Running her fingers through her long hair as she let the air dry it, Lily rose with regret as if breaking some unspeakable bond, and paced slowly back to the shade where her tea waited for her. Catching Shiwezi in her glance, she saw that the younger woman looked away all too quickly, and realized that if she had been having thoughts about Shiwezi, the other had apparently been scrutinizing her at the same time.

Lily laughed in embarrassment—not out loud, but did not bother to try and figure out what Shiwezi might or might not make of her—a woman cursed once and then also absolved?

The hunters came bounding back with a large buck. The midday camp came alive with conversation about the hunt while they made quick work of skinning the animal and searing the meat over the hot coals that Shiwezi stirred up. With some venison in their stomaches, and the rest smoked and tucked in a pouch, the party picked up their separate burdens and proceeded. Mbo, Lily duly noted, carried only the meat.

\*     \*     \*

Crossing the highlands was a 'debilitating adventure,' Lily thought, borrowing a phrase she had often wondered about before in Fitzi-patriki's book. Finally, she felt she was in the process of defining it.

Thick, her head pounding at every step of the way, her feet as weighty as two bricks, she trudged on, what with the hot northern wind lashing dust against all their faces. Lily almost longed for the dull humidity, heavy in the forests.

Above all she missed water, the rushing, flowing, roar of water. It was the anticipation of the Robolo that kept her in step, pressing forward; kept her spirit keen.

But if she grew eager, it became plain that her party grew more and more restless, and Shiwezi listless, her pace dropping off. Lily could feel her behind slowing the pace, the gap between them widening. And Topi in his responsible way would call up ahead. Mbo and Peta would keep going, but Ngobi would stop, his shoulders sagging. He wants his drink, thought Lily. Ngobi would lift off his bundle and sit down, light up the clay pipe which seemed to have become his possession. And Lily would stop to wipe her brow as she called shrilly for the two ahead to stop. At one point when they trudged reluctantly back, perhaps eyeing the pipe, she snapped at Mbo, "You must take some of your bundle back. The weight is slowing her down."

His expression was one of long-suffering, but he took his bundle back. Oddly enough it was Peta who looked insulted, but he said nothing. And they made their way again, flies sticking to their faces—around their eyes and noses.

Shiwezi's pace did not pick up; it was as though she were sick. Worst of all was the sullen silence, the utter lack of song.

Finally they came to a grove of thorn trees, nobody questioning the need to sit in the shade.

Shiwezi unrolled her mat, took the baby off her back and began to nurse him. He too, seemed upset, fussy.

Lily's own head pounded relentlessly, and for awhile she didn't care how long they all sat there. Mbo did not sit, but leaned on his spear, staring off. Ordinarily, they would have been happy to eat up the smoked meat, but no one moved much more than to slurp some water.

This is fever country, thought Lily trying to see where Mbo's gaze focused. Or is it that we are out of place?

Whatever it was, she began to understand that the mood had to do with something else, not simply the heat or a change in atmospheric pressure.

"All right, Mbo," she said, trying to sound contrite, "why is she dragging her feet?"

40

He looked at her in surprise, but couldn't she detect a gleam of triumph in his eyes that said, I have known why all along.

"It is bad magic," he explained simply as if to a novice, which she was, but she would have liked to be humored.

She tried not to bristle. "You mean we might run into someone unfriendly."

He shrugged. She hated it when he shrugged. Indulge me, she wanted to shout, indulge my ignorant mind.

Lily stood up, brushing the dust off her skirt. "Then surely Shiwezi can feel out which way for us to go where there is less badness. She said that she has not seen any other white woman. So let us give a wide berth to this area and seek out the roots of another tributary. Any one we find will drain into the Robolo."

A light came to his eyes; his posture changed as he flashed his teeth. "Ayee. This is good, Ma." His whole attitude towards her changed as he slapped at his comrades to rise up, whistled. Little Mtoli even stopped fussing and began to nurse while watching them all with interested eyes.

"God," muttered Lily, "so that's all it is. We were heading smack into her old stomping ground. Why the hell didn't he say something? I can accept my fate as I must—surprise leopards, possible hostilities—but I'll be damned if I go looking for it."

"Why didn't you say something?" she put to him, as he doled out pieces of meat.

He looked at her, arching his beautiful neck, tilting his arrogant head. "You say to me that you have lifted this curse, but Shiwezi, she is marked now."

"How is she marked?" Lily looked down at Shiwezi who was focused on her baby, letting him suck the juice of the meat off her fingers which she held to his mouth. He smacked his tiny lips.

Mbo made a motion of disgust at Shiwezi's scant clothing as though she were attired top to toe in some inappropriate gown for the occasion.

"Well what am I supposed to do, disguise her?" Lily snorted in exasperation.

41

But that seemed to be exactly his intention. "She is a wife to you now."

"All right," she conceded. "Tell me what to do."

Ah, at last, he seemed to say as his shoulders straightened, the white woman is smartening up. He was glad to tell her what to do. "You must give her cloth and beads. She must make the clothes of a second wife. She must have honor."

"Gladly," Lily tried to mask her exasperation. "Why didn't you just tell me this?"

He shrugged with one shoulder only.

Oh I see it now, she fumed, mouthing to herself what his attitude conveyed: Because I didn't bother to ask! How the bloody hell am I supposed to know what to ask? Would he have just let us walk back on into her former village, all hell break loose, while I stood at the center in my ignorance? Probably he would have! Letting Shiwezi meet her fate all over again. What's it to him anyway? What does he want with a curse around? No wonder we Europeans get into messes. Even I knew enough that Louis Gilbert should have asked some questions or at least seen what was taking place. But here I have been just as blind in my intolerable way.

Wiping the sweat off her brow, she opened one of her trader sacks, greatly relieved, quite sure she had just spared herself an untimely death.

Now what in bloomin' Christian hell does a second wife wear?

She turned over her glass beads to Mbo. "Tell her to take what she needs but that she must give me what she is wearing in exchange. She will have to use the blue I have because I don't have that black-blue kind for the dowry."

But of course—give me your cursed clothing to take back to the fogs of London as a fetish, as a curio. Marriage beadwork: red for the menstruating woman....

What odd fragments of life she picked up unwittingly. Masa's drum, Shiwezi's cast off status as a concubine.

While they settled into a more permanent camp for the rest of the day and night, Lily wrote in her journal; the men smoked, sat in a circle amusing themselves in a game of chance played with three sticks of different lengths. Baby

Mtoli crawled about investigatively, engaging Lily in a shy game of peek-a-boo, and Shiwezi worked up a pattern of col-'or with beads in her new skirt.

And it was during that hot stifling afternoon that Lily came upon another discovery, quite by accident. It began as she sat on a rock, writing, and noticed the button on her sleeve-cuff was loose. She pulled it off in agitation, then began to roll the sleeve neatly up her arm, exposing her skin up to the elbow. She could see how the sun had left freckles even through the cotton fabric.

It was the act of rolling up her sleeve than stunned her, sent a shiver through her as though a sudden cold wind had sprung upon her like the leopard upon Masa. How many times had she rolled up her sleeves in preparation, either to bath her mother or scrub down the sick room? In those moments she had switched from the lady of the house to servant, nursemaid, from the outward pretenses of her family's position in society to the reality of lot in life, her duty. Did all of that follow her even here, sitting in the scant shade under an equatorial sun?

Carefully, deliberately, she unbuttoned her next sleeve and rolled it up to the elbow too. "No longer a lady, nor a scullery maid am I," she announced aloud, "but an explorer looking for another, not quite like myself, in unlikely places." Will she be a woman who rolls up her sleeves? It was hard to imagine. All Lily could imagine her to be was like the women she knew back on the coast, homesick and keeping to the shade.

A brown hand touched her fore-arm. Lily looked up in surprise to find Shiwezi's deep eyes upon her. Certainly, she had grown accustomed to the people wanting to touch her. But Shiwezi did not touch her simply out of curiosity. In her other hand she held a copper bracelet, shaped like a 'C' which she gently fit onto Lily's right wrist with a simple word, "Sa sa." Here.

The metal was warm against her skin, warm from the sun, warm from the arm of another woman. The inner chill deep within Lily, melted. A great sorrow flooded through her—all the pain she had steeled herself with through the

43

years—and she might have wept had she been alone. But she stiffened; she had wept before—enough sniveling.

Here she was enfolded within the bosom of Africa, comforted. By now she had come to equate weeping with European sentimentality, much preferring how the Faung took care of their fear and grief of living—with great wailing, chanting, and throbbing dance. Perhaps they did live with a dangerous, parallel shadow world, a spirit world, but the only shadows she had were those of the past which she was determined to cast aside from her thoughts. Her shadow world was out of place here; deliberately, she had come all this way to create new memory.

She would let the old, lingering pain slip away from her, all of it from the very beginning. She would forget; how she would forget!

## 5.

"You will travel someday too."

These words had hung in Lily's memory from the age of eight on, painfully reminding her that there had been happier times, full of promise before her mother had become bedridden, before Edward had gone away to school, and before her father had travelled further away to come back less and less.

The words had been spoken by a woman whose statuesque presence had flooded the Bascombe house with life for a time. Lily remembered her as someone who used the word "Antiquities" a great deal, and was someone who had actually seen the pyramids. 'Auntie Vanessa,' Lily was allowed to call her, and although she was no blood relation at all, Lily would happily have traded any or all her relatives to claim Auntie Vanessa as her own. In her soul she did.

It was not that Auntie Vanessa had paid a great deal of attention to her, but daily she had given her a moment, even a moment, of direct attention which Lily had swallowed like an elixir.

Once in the parlor, dressed as she was in raw silk of a dusty rose color, she had taken Lily to sit in her lap. Vividly, Lily remembered, how Auntie Vanessa lifted her up into her lap, looking down as the silk skirt rode up to reveal high suede boots, a deep reddish color with well worn creases. "Ah yes," Auntie Vanessa said in acknowledgement, "the soles of those boots have touched the the steps of the Acropolis, the paw of the Sphinx." And then she laughed, her head back. Watching her from inches away, Lily saw how the hair from her bun strayed loose, how she had crinkles around

45

her bright eyes, and how her skin was not at all pale like Mother's.

"Next we will go up the Nile, won't we?" The question was directed at Lily's father who hovered nearby. "We shall search out the source of the Nile and end up in the unexplored forests of the African equator! Won't we? And in these boots, I shall be the first white woman to tread there." As though she had told a joke, her laughter mocked the dark room.

Lily turned to look at her father. He stood, arms folded, except for the finger that played along his moustache. There was a long pause before he answered with a dry laugh.

It was then that Vanessa whispered softly against the rim of Lily's ear, "You will travel someday too."

With a cough, Lily's father interrupted, holding out a paper packet of medicine. "Come now, take this up to your mother, there's a good girl."

Lily did not want to go up to her mother who had retreated with a headache, and for a moment she did not move, could not bear to be dismissed from that seat, so full of radiant warmth with Auntie Vanessa's arms firmly around her. Her father rattled the packet in irritation as he handed it to her, and suddenly Auntie Vanessa's arms loosened. "Go on," he said.

Down the years Lily often wondered what would have happened had she stayed seated in Auntie Vanessa's lap, if those arms had not let go, and she had not gone to her mother. She dreamed again and again all her childhood years of having stayed there—of how this magical woman who had visited so briefly took her away so that the soles of Lily's own shoes could also touch the Antiquities.

As it was, she fled that day, stopping at the foot of the stairway to look back through the parlor door, and saw her father bend over, one of his hands on that silken knee, the other running up the booted calf as Auntie Vanessa laughed. Only then had Lily turned away, flushing as she bounded up the stairs. On the landing, in semi-darkness, she ran into Edward who stood there leaning over the railing.

He spoke to her bitterly then. "Do you know who she is,

46

that one? She is a Duchess, and she's very rich. She met father in Egypt, and now he's going to be the doctor in her party. He is abandoning us, Lily, all of us—for her. That means I am to be sent away to school now. There won't be a tutor here anymore for me, you know, so don't be surprised if that's the end of your lessons."

Lily said nothing in response. She had no doubt by the way he spoke, that what he said was true.

Later that night unable to sleep, she stole downstairs, some deep, unnameable desperation driving her. Stopping in the hallway, she saw the door of her father's library open. Tip-toeing in, she paused next to a chair which was pushed away from the table and left there as though the reader had been interrupted—distracted. Next to the chair were two upright, leather boots. Stooping down, Lily felt them, the fine leather soft with wear, taking one into her arms like she might pick up the kitchen cat while she sat sobbing.

Only later, wiping away tears, had she climbed up onto the chair to inspect the open book on the library table. Keeping the place, she closed the book and read the embossed title: *The Source of the Nile*. Turning back to the open page, she read as best she could in the darkness, so that once again when she had the chance, she could find this book. She had made out a word underlined, a name in the text: Fitzpatrick, not the author of the book, but someone who had written extensively about *Equatorial Africa and the Dark Continent*. She sounded out the words, powerful in their mystique.

Everything that Edward had said on the landing came true. Lily found herself alone in the house in the care of—or caring for—her mother who became a demanding invalid in her seclusion, while the country cook, Audrey, kept the house going.

In the years ahead it was only in the kitchen, bright and warm, where Lily could find some life—and in her secret journeys to her father's library. She never found *The Source of the Nile* but even so, with the help of that brief inspection of Auntie Vanessa's book, that inadvertent, secret glimpse, Lily was able to find the works of Clive Fitzpatrick on one of the library shelves. Curling up in a library chair, she would read and dream. In her youthful fantasies she created hazardous journeys towards nebulous watery goals. What a disappointment to discover from Edward that Lake Victoria had already been established as the Nile's beginning, shortly before she was born. What a triumph to then learn that Fitzpatrick wished to seek it out from the West coast of Africa, something he had not accomplished before his untimely death from an infected wound.

But by the time she was in her twenties, Lily had long given up the dream that one day her father would come home and tell her that she too, was going to travel with him, and she had given up the hope that Auntie Vanessa would come back again and claim her, a companion for the voyage. In one of her father's rare, formal letters, he announced Aunt Vanessa's death by dysentery in Turkey, and that he was becoming a doctor to a company in the Orient. How old had she been then, fifteen? All hope gone.

Night after night though the years, Lily bolted the doors of the house before retiring. Night after night she watched how she locked herself in, stranded and forgotten.

Then, all of a sudden, at the age of thirty, after all the years of imagination and will held captive, Lily found herself free to live beyond her books, free to leave the confines of the library and her home. It was some time before she recognized the opportunity. She had lived for so many years by her mother's sickbed with a book to keep her mind occupied that it took her by surprise to find her mother dead—no more sickbed to sit at—and to get word that her father had died at sea on a voyage.

All this happened within the space of a few months. But only when her father's solicitor came to see her to discuss the will did it become clear that she was no longer bound to household and nursing duties as she had been for her entire adult life.

Of course there was her brother to consider, especially since he inherited the bulk of the estate, but even so, a handsome enough sum was set aside in her name—enough to buy a cottage by the sea, if she chose. A sum of money to use as she pleased.

It did not occur to her at first to use the money in any particular way; after all, there was the mourning period to get through, and then the task of making sure Edward was set up in the house. She knew she would be free of this familial duty as soon as he made his marriage arrangements final. But Edward was slow, if not disinterested in the idea of pinning himself down to any one particular young lady. And so Lily found herself still very much absorbed in mind journeys to various place in the world through her father's travel and geography books. All the while the clock ticked away the hollow hours in the front hall. The place she went back to again and again was Africa.

She never talked about it, but then no one asked. Edward didn't care. As long as his dinner was on time and his tea brought to him in the morning, what his sister did in the library was of no consequence to him whatsoever. Often he dined out at his club and didn't return home at all in the evening, while Lily spread out rudimentary maps on the table, candles holding down all the corners and traced rivers with her forefinger, that finger stopping here and there to tap.

When Edward announced one breakfast that he was not getting married to Miss Catherine Norwood, his third engagement in as many years, she did feel panic, yes, but just for a moment. Choking on her hot porridge, she sat in silence waiting for him to go into his usual sort of explanation of how this one again was not suitable or that the family wasn't, when he changed tack completely, and announced he was going to China.

"For how long?" She asked almost inaudibly.

"Oh for a year or so," he answered, brushing toast crumbs from his neat moustache. "You are free to come or go as you please while I'm gone. Certainly you can always stay with Aunt Deidre if you wish."

"No, no, that won't be necessary," Lily said quickly, dreading the very idea of assuming any duties involving her crippled aunt. "I shall be going to Africa."

"Africa?" Edward's mouth twisted slightly as he paled. By the look in his eye she wondered if he were not remembering

49

Vanessa. She waited, breathless, certain that he was about to say something, but he scraped his chair as he stood up. "Do you think that's wise?"

"Wiser than going to be with Aunt Deidre."

"Ah, quite so, quite so—as long as you return by the time I do and have the house open and ready. Not to mention collecting your stipend."

"What?"

His mouth twisted again. "The solicitor didn't tell you? If you don't collect your annual stipend personally, it defaults to me automatically. Now I needn't have told you—I assumed you knew." With that, he left to go about his business, not bothering to ask her what part of Africa she had in mind. But then, she hadn't asked him where he was going in China either.

The dull room with its dark furnishings took on a new glow in his wake. Her heart skipped, as though sunshine had broken through the heavy morning fog. A year of freedom would be like a lifetime.

She was going to Africa, to the 'Dark Continent.' The idea that it was a dark place amused her when all the maps pointed out quite clearly that a tropical sun beat down upon that place. What could be darker than the morning-room? Slowly, she rose from the table and reverting to her servitude, she cleared away the breakfast things, thinking that shortly she would be counting the days until her voyage.

How did one go about booking a passage?

Taking the breakfast dishes through to the kitchen, she was accosted by a loud harangue on the part of Audrey, directed at a fast retreating figure.

"Bugger off! You're nothing but a bastard and a disgrace to yer fine family name...." she was yelling, what with the meat cleaver held aloft, eyes wild with fury, her hair falling from its pins.

Lily shook her head. Undoubtedly, Audrey was after Durgie, the butcher's son again. There was never a dull moment in the kitchen; even in its most dull moment, the kettle on the stove would be steaming, full tilt.

"Lord, I don't know," Audrey turned back. "Doesn't he

50

think I know rotten meat when I see it. Bloody scoundrel, he ís, that one."

Lily set down the tray on the large kitchen table. "I'm going to Africa."

Audrey who was about to make a pie and still red in the face, dropped the cleaver on the table; stared across at Lily. "What?" She said, blowing a strand of hair out of her face at the same time.

"I've cleared it with Edward already. As a matter of fact, he is going to China."

"Good God, get me some tea would ye?" Audrey decided to take a seat on the kitchen bench near the stove.

Lily proceeded to comply, filling a tea cup from a pot keeping warm near the stove. They had done this many times for each other. In fact, Audrey was the only person Lily ever really talked to about anything. It was from Audrey that she had learned there was any zest to living, any color and heat to language. After all, Audrey had raised her as one of her own brood—teaching her the tasks she knew: how to pluck a chicken, how to help birth a calf, how to boil the laundry, how to bake bread. And even now, she still went once a month on a Sunday to Audrey's cottage, leaving one of Audrey's nieces to look after things at the Bascombe residence. Surrounded by Audrey's children and the grandchildren who tumbled about, eating fresh bread or yorkshire pudding in the crowded, low cottage rooms, Lily felt truly at home, whether it was the talk of crops, breed of chickens or the latest news about the Queen. But she also knew she was not truly one with them. Servant and yet daughter to her mother, she was still of another class and expectation, one that left her moored. Isolated.

She had never talked to her dear Audrey about Africa or what she read in her books, though Audrey was certainly aware of Lily's pastime, walking in on the maps spread out, picking up books from the floor in the kitchen. In that area Lily remained alone, out of touch with others who might have been able to converse with her, and had little way of knowing how to reach out. Certainly her own blood relations weren't helpful. Lily taught herself, buying the latest magazine's to find out what ideas or politics brewed in her nation. If I can go off and do something like Auntie Vanessa did, then I shall be interesting, and I shall have something to say, be someone to take note of.

By announcing her intentions to Audrey, the reality of her scheme became much more binding than anything she could have felt with Edward. Her longtime cohort took the cup of tea and sipped loudly, waiting.

"I don't know how I'm going to do it yet, but I do have a sum of money I can put toward the endeavor. I thought I would trade my way into the interior, bring back curios, and sell writings about my expeditions when I get back. Perhaps I can even establish a trade route; I hear rubber is brought out—I can see, perhaps I can go even further the next time, once I'm taken seriously."

Audrey looked at her, non-plussed. "Blimey. You gone daft on me."

"No." Lily smiled her wan, guarded smile. "I'll go."

"Savin' up this plan all these years have you? I always used to wonder what you was dreaming about, lass. But it's as sure as courting death, if you ask me."

"I've thought of that. But this is death, Audrey. This is my death here."

"Aye, that it is. I won't argue with ye there. All these years seein' to yer mother, and not having found yerself a man to marry, at that." Audrey did not bother to ask the obvious— what is to become of me; she merely sighed, holding her tea cup between her knees.

"I'll come back when Edward does, of course. And the house is yours to live in, and take care of."

"Aye, and who do I cook fer?"

"Bring your relations in. Your niece and her husband— they need a place. This house could use some children around to take out the gloom, and they would love the garden which is all because of your doing anyway."

"That's not proper, Miss. What would your brother say?"

"The hell with him." Lily said heatedly. "When has anything been proper here? You're more family to me than my relative, and I don't forget that you raised me. If you feel you need to, cover the furniture, close off the parlor...."

"Do you mean to do this—go to Africa?"

"Yes."

"Good Lord. I believe you will."

"And I will come back too, so don't you worry. I must be back in time for Edward's return."

"Aye."

Edward made no attempts to help her with arrangements, but she coaxed him into telling her his travel plans in bits and pieces over dinner, until she felt confident enough to approach the task for herself.

She booked a passage on the *Fourth Wind* which was bound for the Cape of Good Hope, the day after Edward was to depart for the Orient, drinking a late night brandy with Audrey to celebrate.

Under *reasons or purpose of voyage* she wrote: *to visit with relatives in the colony.* And as an after-thought added mentally—especially my long departed Aunt Vanessa.

As for Edward—he didn't know, nor did he ask anything.

Counting the days, Lily packed quietly, buying beads herself, tobacco and liquor through Audrey's nephew-in-law— small quantities at a time from different sources. Likewise, he procured a pistol, taking her out to a place in the country for shooting. "Right between the eyes," he told her. She found that she had a steady aim.

With Audrey and her niece's help, Lily made a dozen light collarless, cotton shirts, each embroidered with her initials, and a set of pinstripe skirts, giving up the idea of petticoats for simple pantaloons with only four ruffles of lace at the ankles—rather than all the way up to the knee.

And in spite of Audrey's persuasions to take two whalebone corsets, Lily decided she'd make do with only one. For footwear she had two pairs of sturdy walking shoes made, her romantic memories of high, red-leather boots having long ago been dismissed as impractical.

Additional items included three leather-bound journals, a ruler, two bundles of carefully wrapped rice paper, two pens, three bottles of blue india-ink, and a packet of twenty-five nibs, various carefully copied maps and notations.

She counted the days until she was free. Africa and its *unexplored forests of the equator* called to her soul like Aunt Vanessa's whisper so long ago.

Audrey accompanied her by train to South Hampton for the embarkation, dutifully posting Lily's farewell letter of explanation to her uncle and solicitor after the boat departed.

Had Lily worried about the matter of being chaperoned—which she had—she was soon comforted. Her fellow passengers assumed she was a missionary. She was used to playing along with people's assumptions about her. She even took to carrying a small leather-bound Bible along with her on her deck strolls—not her own 'good book' by any means, but one she borrowed from the small chapel. There were missionaries bound for the south, who took it upon themselves to engage her in prayer and conversation, and she bore up stoically, answering their questions with short non-committal phrases she was beginning to pick up, grateful for her few experiences of evensong. Otherwise, she thought, I'd be considered too much of a heathen .

It was the Captain Lowell who saved her, inviting her to his table for dinner one evening during particularly rough seas. Most of the passengers had retreated to their cabins, too sick to eat, but for some reason she seemed to have found her sea legs, and even had an appetite. Conversation was formal—sea stories, her inquiries about people he knew, where they had gone, what had happened to them. When he offered her some after dinner port, and saw that she accepted, he laughed, and in that instant, although she didn't know it right away, he became her friend.

Captain Lowell had broken through her ability to camouflage. "I knew you were no missionary!" said he. "Though you have been very good at it. No god-fearing missionary would drink my port—though I have met one other exception."

Embarrassed, yet pleased, Lily put down her glass quickly, lingered with her fingers still upon it, then raised it once again, looking at him across the rim.

She found that he was well-versed with Fitzpatrick's writings, a man whom he called 'a pompous arse' much to her delight.

54

And he listened with keen interest to her plans about exploring possible trade routes and charting more accurate maps inland as no one ever had, not even Audrey. She revelled in her stroke of luck as she walked the decks late at night in the chilly sea air. Someone took her seriously at last, could enjoy her pursuit from his captain's chair at the head of his table. "Let me be so bold as to make a slight suggestion," he said. "I advise you to take apart your revolver if you wish to go into French territory on the south side of Lake Fitzpatrick—I'll show you how to do it, and put it back together right—otherwise the officials at port of entry will confiscate it. If you have it in pieces, hidden among various items in your luggage, you will experience no problems.

Don't indicate that you are taking liquor to trade. Speak of your store as gifts to your colonial hosts along the way. There's quite a nasty issue brewing about giving liquor to the natives these days. It has changed since Fitzpatrick's time. Once you're away from the coast, you won't have to care."

He had winked once. "You can return that Bible now, unless you think it might give you words of comfort someday."

Quietly, she replaced the Bible in the chapel, and took her meals with him for the remainder of the voyage. The only impatience she felt was for that first glimpse of African shores. Even when she knew she was still days away, she would lean on the deck railing and gaze out at the limitless horizon of ocean white-caps. She was used to waiting, but now her body burned in the waiting. She wept in her bitter longing, great salty tears, as the great bronze propellers of the ship churned the waters deep below her, insistently, insistently.

# 6.

Time stood still in the heat up on the high plateau as Lily and her party trudged on, the flies sticking to everything. All the buzzing blended in with an even greater hum of swarming locusts clattering among the tall grasses as they feasted on the ripening seed.

Mbo, during one of his forays found the party a shady spot near a spring where Shiwezi built three reed and grass huts. True, Ngobi did prepare the saplings and provided her with sinew to lash the frames together, otherwise, the men either went out to hunt or else sat about in the shade smoking the clay pipe. Here they would stay until Shiwezi finished beading her skirt.

Throughout the days Lily went her own way, taking short treks about the country side, picking plant specimens to come back and ask questions about. In the morning and evening she took the simple pleasure of watching the wary game come to the spring's small water hole. Privately, she was glad to camp because she was menstruating.

And all the while, Shiwezi worked on her beading until at last, her new skirt was done. How many days had it taken?—five perhaps, by Lily's careful accounting. She wondered with great consternation whether she had not lost a day here or there, what with her visions of arriving back at the coast off by a month or two. It didn't help that her pocket watch which she had meticulously wound every night, stopped one mid-morning when she was out walking. Aghast, she realized she had missed winding it the night before. And left with the choice of creating an arbitrary time dependent upon her calculations of the sun, she abandoned all care of her timepiece and stowed it away in her portmanteau.

Her calendar remained clear by her diary because she knew she wrote in it at least once a day, and she always put the date. She counted back in it, all the days of her expedition out from the Oguye, and discovered she had written one date twice in the turning of a page. Had she written twice that day? Did those events happen on the same day? She wracked her brain, going over every occurrence, the pivotal moment always being when the leopard jumped out at Masa. She would begin there. In what sequence had things happened after that. Slowly she would go over her accounts of the journey, then doubt what she had written.

But I cannot doubt what I have recorded! Her head reeled with the thought that she could let this fine line of reality—words on a page—stand as a distortion. And yet she would count back the days, fix her stare on the double date, find herself once again along the forest path just before Masa's quick cry of surprise.

That she had lost her sense of time, that she could not be quite sure, disturbed her. She tried to pass it off , but she was uneasy, restless about moving on, getting into a pace again. At last Shiwezi finished her skirt, and they all took on a new attitude of anticipation.

Their last night by the spring, Mbo built an enormous fire, throwing on wood almost in a frenzy. His actions did not go without notice among the men; they began to banter with him, edging him on, Topi taking to beating an empty water gourd with sticks and setting a rhythm.

Lily watched them from the low doorway of her hut, sitting on a small mat she had made for herself out of ropes of grass knotted together. Although her body was quiet, she too was aroused by the fire, taking in the orange reflection of fire on the gleaming bronze bodies of the Faung.

Topi began to entertain with a story. Slowly she realized what he was playing out, her eyes widening in horror.

First, he crouched, feline, his voice in his throat, now like a purr, now like a snarl. He sprang upon the large log the men had dragged into the fire circle, crouched, his whole body sinewy and taut. He had become a wild cat, flicking his buttocks as though he indeed, had a tail. How narrow his eyes became, as they focused on his prey.

Just beyond his reach, Ngobi sauntered, his whole manner changing, no longer his own but someone else's—in the way that he placed his feet as he walked with an exaggerated weight so that they splayed out. It was in the way he carried his imaginary burden, what with his head cocked slightly, his right shoulder hunched a bit.

Lily had forgotten, until this moment of renewed and painful reminder. It was Masa who walked there. The way he carried his burden was due to an old wound he had received once while hunting warthog, having been gored in the shoulder. Ngobi made much of this caricature, ridiculing Masa who had been so foolish as to be gored by a warthog, so foolish that he would be....

Topi sprang with a snarl, leapt with as much grace and fury as the leopard, his whole body a spring uncoiling explosively.

A cry rent the air.

Was it Ngobi? Was it Lily as she jumped to her feet?

Topi lay full length on top of Ngobi whose eyes were wide in mock horror, the veins of his neck like ropes. And then they were rolling on the ground, rollicking with laughter. Mbo who had been nursing the pipe as he squatted was beside himself with mirth, collapsed on the ground too. Even Shiwezi on her mat with her sleeping bay at her side, shook with laughter in her belly and breasts.

"Stop it!" Lily shouted, her voice shrill and echoing into the dark vastness of the night. Her body was taut with strain, sweat trickling down her temples. "Stop it, I say."

"Ho," came Mbo's quick, but subdued reply, even as he picked himself up slowly. With the slightest flick of his hand the others fell silent, Ngobi and Topi still heaving deeply where they lay sprawled on the ground.

Lily looked at Mbo sternly. "Masa is dead. You yourself carry his fetish to take it back to its rightful place."

"Mmm, mm." Mbo clucked in his throat, not disagreeing.

"How can you dishonor his spirit so?"

Mbo made no answer, but took her words as an order for

all levity to cease. "I will make tea, Ma."

Lily sighed in distress, retreating to her hut where she fought back hot tears, and also the hoard of mosquitoes driven there by the smoke from the fire. Couldn't the infernal insects leave her alone; she was bleeding enough as it was.

"I don't know what day it is." She sobbed into the canvas pack that served as her pillow. How could she have made such an error? Had Mbo showed her how the ticks sit on a blade of grass the same day or the next? She could see the blade clearly in her mind. Had the grass been wet with dew or rain? How could she possibly have written a new date incorrectly? She had to trust herself, count back the days until her previous cycle, count forward, but even that was not certain because in all the changes to her body, that regularity had changed too, becoming infrequent. Oh God, she sighed, if I am to establish a trade route or ever write about my adventures for fame and fortune, I'm going to have to survive it all first.

For the first time she felt truly homesick, longing for Audrey's familiar cooking, for the press of Audrey's grandchildren about her, for the taste of new, yeasted bread. But then she remembered her family's cold, dark house.

Presently, Mbo was squatting at her door, proffering a steaming tin mug. "Tea time, Ma," he said in the same cheerful tones that any good mission boy could mimic the first day on the job.

Rallying herself, she crawled out, not caring to be dignified. After all, she was miserable. She had to get back to the protective cloud of smoke.

Mbo grunted in satisfaction at having coaxed her out. He began to speak to her gently in his tongue. "Topi; this man, he is a storyteller. He is very wise in his stories and bring us the leopard. He brings Masa out of Ngobi...."

"But you make fun of him!" Lily retorted, knowing she failed in her expression because she only knew the word for 'goad' as used by the Faung when they toyed with a crocodile in the river.

"Yes, Ma." He shook his head in satisfaction.

She shrugged helplessly. What was the use? She was in

their world, she reminded herself. What right did she have to question that they laugh—challenging and appeasing—in the grim face of death?

# 7.

Finding the first signs of wetland brought on an elation to the small party, dusty and tired from the trek across the dry plateau. They first found a marsh, full of scarlet ibis and white heron, which seemed to be spring-fed because the water was cold. Mbo pointed out one spot where the water bubbled up.

So, the beginnings of the Robolo at last. Lily sighed. Or at least a tributary thereof. Any river life would also mean people, and that in turn, could mean anything. If her Faung companions were nervous, she could only hope that as usual, her appearance would be such a novelty that it would divert any hostile receptions. One couldn't count on it, but, so far, things had worked out. She had to remain confident that if the negotiation of her Faung guides were to fail, her supply of liquor might suffice.

They began a slow descent into forest, following the course of a tumbling stream over boulders and massive tree roots. Once again there were signs of monkeys and birds, as leaves and fruits tumbled down at them from the restless movement in the trees above.

And then came the waterfall. Approaching it from above, the roar was unmistakable and thrilling to Lily. She stopped in a cloud of mist at the brink and watched the water tumble in a thin white wisp curling down perhaps a hundred feet or so far below. Pausing for refreshment with the others, she sat on a great wet rock, mesmerized, while Mbo began to scout out a way to climb down into the wider valley below.

In the mist and spray of the waterfall were gigantic fern fronds and large green leafy plants with purple veins. These

61

clung to the cracks between rocks like a clusters of huge, vibrant green moths, their wings trembling. At any moment she almost expected them to take flight

Mbo came back with his typical exclamations of disgust and impossibility. Ngobi had already lit up the clay pipe. And Lily was still entranced, forgetting that she had actually worried about what day it was. She smiled. If and when she ever got back to the coast, she had no doubt she would be informed; she would be like any other of Captain Lowell's mosquito ridden explorers stumbling forth from the interior, sputtering: "What day is it?" followed by a long and reverent: "God save the Queen."

The passage down giant, slimy boulders was arduous enough without bundles, so they had to make use of what meagre rope Lily had to lower her goods from one slippery rock level to another, relying on roots for had-holds. Mtoli, on the other hand, went down easily on his mother's back—she having determined to leave the men to their work—and when at last, they all made it down, Shiwezi was already bathing him in the pool below the waterfall, his gurgles of delight blending with that of the water.

Lily looked over all the packs, afraid of any broken liquor bottles, but everything had made it intact. So she suggested that they go hunting to find a suitable pelt or hide to present to their potential hosts. One leopard skin was prize enough for a chief, and the antelope hides would certainly be presentable though ordinary. They needed a more unusual addition, if they were to be taken seriously as traders. She knew the men wanted nothing more for their entertainment. Besides, she had her own needs: she wanted to bathe.

"Mbo?" She queried, "Are there any snakes here?"

He flashed his sharp white teeth, grinning in amusement, and in anticipation of using the spear he tossed from hand to hand lightly, "No snakes, Ma. Here the water it is too fast."

He was about to lope off with the others when he said, quite soberly, "Here there is 'Ntu, the spirit. It lives there in the deep part." He waved his hand at the shadows behind the falls. By his intonation he was definitely referring to a female spirit. His eyes widened., his brow wrinkling up. "She

does not harm you, this one, but yes, she plays with you!"
And with that, he was off.

Plays with me? Lily pondered, removing the clips from her
hair. Once again the concept was more that the spirit might
toy with her like the many tricksters the Faung believed in. A
benevolent spirit at any rate. She took comfort in that as she
pulled off her shoes and stockings, dabbling her naked feet
in the cool eddies. Toy with me, eh? Summing up her courage, she waded thigh deep into the water, taking along her
still swamp-sullied clothes and a hoarded stock of soiled
menstrual rags to beat on the rocks, and clean. Gazing up at
the waterfall, she stuck out a hand to feel the sharp sting of
the droplets. Like needles they pummelled her as she moved
her body into its body, growing numb until she gasped for
air. When she emerged, she had only one wish and that was
to remove her shirt, her skirt, everything that encumbered
her. Could she? The men had disappeared into the forest;
Shiwezi too had slipped away to gather fruits.

Deliberately, even anxiously, Lily unbuttoned her shirt
and pulled it off, but her yellowed chemise, her laced-up corset, her pantaloons rebuked her.

In broad daylight? Here? She shrank from the idea for a
belabored moment. Did she truly dare, what, and exposed
her mottled skin, ugly with freckles and inflamed insect
bites?

There was no one about, and yet it was as though all the
unseen eyes of the forest creatures were upon her in a
hushed expectancy.

"Bloody hell, who's to stop me? God save the Queen!"

She pulled off her clothes, draping them over handy rocks
and leaves, laughing as she untied her bodice, pulled loose
the tight laces, then plunged into the water, laughing because the current chilled and yet enveloped her. Methinks,
sure as not, that I have found Margery *Pool* ! Or do I pre-
sume too much?

Captain Lowell said Margery had 'gone bush.' Lily wondered if she herself were not going the same half-crazed
route. With time flowing out of her control like the water that
swirled around her, it was unavoidable. A wave of tension

washed over her—that she should dress quickly and be done with it. But the water teased her, tugged at her arms and legs, holding her there.

And so she stayed, floating on her back as she gazed up at the giant green and purple moths and the wet rock face, the cascade of water sweeping down.

How long did she hold herself there before reluctantly pulling away, cleansed, her skin covered with goose bumps for the first time since she came to Africa? Slowly she began to gather up her wet garments. The corset was missing. Gone. Looking all about the rocks and ferns revealed nothing. Standing with her hands on her hips, she stared downstream at the white water tumbling over the rocks below.

Yes, she had been toyed with. A joke, a joke: just like that, her bodice had disappeared. It was hard for her to accept. She could imagine a monkey sidling up, bounding over the rocks to scoop it away. More likely the water had taken it when she wasn't looking. It was the only bodice she had, what with its stained, satin panels and bone stays, stiff lacy-edged half-cups which supported her breasts. She was used to it like one gets used to wearing armor as a matter of habit, a matter of form. More than once she thought it was her corset that kept her standing. Now there was nothing to do about it.

What's to help keep your head up? She spoke to herself in a voice much like Audrey's. She tried to console herself by admitting that she didn't need such an personal accoutrement here in the interior—one less thing to sweat in. But what about when she got back to the coast? Damn it, but this bloody jungle had way of tearing bits and pieces from her—first stealing away her certainty and concept of time, now sweeping her underwear down towards the Robolo.

Naked, she waded out, carrying her clean, wet clothes which she spread on rocks high above the water before rummaging to find her last remaining set of clothes, sans bodice. When she ever met up with Margery Poole, she'd have to remember to stand up straight. How could she be a legitimate representative of civilization if she did not? ...Pieces missing, not a hair on her head in place what with her stock of hair-

64

pins dwindling too.

For the moment she wanted her bodice back very badly, and there wasn't even anyone to complain to. She realized she was lonely, a most irritating discovery. Lonely and very naked. Why was she in this place? To find some lost white woman?

When she had set out to travel in Africa, she had felt an openness, a sense of anticipation at whatever might lie in her path. Why had that infernal Captain brought it upon himself to charge her with the duty of seeing certain papers to a certain woman who didn't even want to be found? Now here she was, bent upon some task which she hadn't asked for, hadn't ever thought of wanting, and more probable than not, would fail at. Colonials and missionaries were easy enough to leave behind; she had grown to prefer the Faung, ever intrigued by the way they saw and interpreted their world. Why did she want to find this woman? The purpose infuriated her all the more because she knew she would be bitterly disappointed now, not to find her. It was as though her long-time, childish goal of finding the source of the Nile had now materialized into a person, no thanks to the captain. 'Miss Poole,' of all things—and looking vaguely like Aunt Vanessa with her mocking laughter and silly red boots. A joke, a joke.

Many times as she had fallen asleep to the hum of mosquitoes in her ears, she had imagined giving the two gifts, tins of the finest quality tobacco and tea, to Margery Poole. And then, the bundle of letters and money as though it were to be some great triumph, some pinnacle of accomplishment. Bah!

For the first time, Lily spat in disgust as she had seen the Faung do—a wad of spittle between her narrow, pink feet.

# 8.

"Ah, civilization at last!" Lily exclaimed as she and her party stumbled across a fetish in their path. A small statue, it stood chest high because of the rock pedestal beneath. Carved out of dark wood, perhaps ebony, the figure was armless, bulbous and mostly two elongated heads, each looking in opposing directions. Inlays of beaten brass indicated necklaces on one and a head-dress on the other. No doubt a sentinel, Lily decided as she made a quick sketch, a spirit, not so much on guard against intruders like herself, but keeping watch on the spirits of the forest. The deliberately exposed teeth in the grimace of the outward-looking face was like that of a gargoyle; it defied entry. The inward-looking face was expressionless by contrast—placid with a hint of sorrow in the way the carver had slanted the eyes downward.

Mbo was used to her close scrutiny of fetishes. He made his own observation, by looking over her shoulder at her pencil renditions, noises issuing from his throat, comments out the side of his mouth, eliciting interested 'Mm mm's in response from Peta and the others. Shiwezi stood at a distance, wary, Mtoli peeking around her.

Oil and fruit stains on the double heads indicated frequent offerings. Lily finished up her sketch, then pulling out her tailor tape-measure, took the dimensions, all the while pondering what proper tribute to leave in exchange for being allowed to pass unharmed.

Topi was already hanging a civet's paw around the fetish's neck, using grass twine he had wound, the paw having come from one of a pair of cats the hunters had killed and skinned.

A plug of tobacco would do, Lily decided, asking Mbo to bring out a pouch. Before long the party was underway again, on their best behavior, if not edgy, and expecting to meet up with people at any time; they didn't sing. It was time for Masa to set up a rhythm and a song of the party's intentions, more importantly, not to come as a surprise to anyone.

The undergrowth was thick; Mbo pulled his scythe from its sheath along his hip, and began slashing back the overhanging vegetation. Lily understood that the vegetation had been left this way on purpose, and she wasn't surprised when they came upon further statues barring the way. Specifically, a circle of statues with elaborate screens of grass in the way, like ambushes. She had seen these screens before; breaking through one was liable to bring down a hail of rocks, perhaps even a spear.

As Lily proceeded to place another plug of tobacco on the central stone that stood in the path, Mbo took the drum from her personal pack. Resolutely taking on the vacated role of drummer, he beat out an inquiry, a greeting, a trader's call.

Often such trading, especially by parties from afar, meant the trading of wives. Lily hoped there wouldn't be too much interest in Shiwezi. She knew she wasn't above scrutiny herself, even with the immunity of being white, dressed in peculiar garb, and with a strange and elementary way of talking. Her task was to tantalize and dazzle any new audience with tobacco and trinkets as soon as possible while her onlookers not only inspected her goods, but also her physical aspects as well—hands on. She knew perfectly well that plenty of hair clips disappeared at times like these.

Bracing herself, she hoped that Mbo wasn't advertising wives of any sort. It was with his people that she had been introduced to the language and a great deal of their customs. Now came the real challenge—presenting herself with what she had learned. Would the leopard skin, the antelope and civet hides be enough of an offering to the chief so that she could do business?

In the third pause of Mbo's refrain, they were answered. Perhaps a mile away? Even though Lily had straightened her back, set her chin stalwartly, her breath caught. The answering rhythm was fast, straightforward. The village was in some sort of celebration, and their presence had been ascertained.

"Spied on us already?" Lily was curious. Mbo probably knew they had, but she had detected no signs of tension from him, none of his keen hand-twitching along the shaft of his spear. Of course not; he had been hacking away the bush.

Bolder, Mbo set up a rhythm and began to sing a list of attributes, in particular about Lily—*a woman from the tribe that comes out of the water.* Undoubtedly, some of the men of the village would have had dealings with white male traders; all of them were the *fish people from the great waters.*

An advance party from the chief came out to greet them, dancing down the path.

"Let us hope, Mbo," Lily muttered under her breath, "that your cousin's cousin of her mother's aunt did not leave gambling debts unpaid here."

The chief sat in the village clearing upon his three-legged throne, his attendants in position, his wives seated in a cluster on grass mats to the side. He seemed to be in a great state of excitement.

"He say he knows of your coming," Mbo informed her, looking equally as baffled as she. "From the river, they have received a sign...."

"A sign?" Lily pushed passed him as a group of dancers leapt into the open arena, presenting the item the chief wanted her very much to see. Intrigued, Lily approached the group, trying to keep an open mind for whatever animal entrails, monkey skull of other bony horror that might await her approval.

One dancer emerged suddenly from the group, as if pushed forward. On his head like an eyeless mask was a stained satin corset, half unstrung, upside down, and with the breast cups flapping over his cheeks.

"That's bloody well ridiculous!" Lily swayed backwards, trying to regained her balance and composure. Chagrined, feeling the blood rush to her face, she burst into a shrill laugh. "That's my—that's...." She turned to a non-plussed

Mbo who had never set his eyes upon her bodice before. What a perfect fetish, whalebone stays protruding, cotton strings unravelling. So perhaps the satin was of a tighter weave—it would have to do as a facsimile of the grass fabric the Faung used for masks. She reeled. "Tell the chief, yes indeed, it is my pleasure that he should have the mask, delivered so for him by the river spirit that has toyed with me. Tell him that to honor him and a successful round of trading, Shiwezi will brew an extraordinary beer, and that I have some gifts as well. Now let us hope that my second-wife knows how to come through for us."

The promise of a brew meant that Lily was settled in the village for a few days.

Graciously, the chief presented her with a hut, but if she had had the assumption that, at last, she would have some privacy, she was mistaken. All night long she heard the rustle of footsteps, the whispers of voices outside as eyes peered through each and every crack. Not bothering to undress, or even to remove her boots, she arranged all her packs to make up some sort of bed. Throwing a woven mat across them, and with her hat for a pillow, she lay down to try and find some sleep, feeling like a queen who must sleep in the presence of curious courtiers.

The task of brewing beer entailed bartering for wild grains and particular roots which varied according to closely guarded recipes which in turn, varied on texture and degree of bitterness. Shiwezi took on her task with a stoic dignity befitting her role. Lily assisted her more as an onlooker writing notes than as a cantankerous, bossy first-wife who customarily did all the supervising, and vied for all the credit.

Mbo took Shiwezi's beer-brewing time as good excuse to accept an offer to go off hunting. She was more or less left in the hands of the youths of the village, rangy lads who were as eager to amuse her as they were of touching her, as most everyone did sooner or later. These boys were especially intrigued by her freckles.

Lily pinched her forearm and in her stumbling Faung said, "I am looking for a woman with skin like this, like mine."

69

All around her, heads nodded and shook in interest, amid rapid discussion back and forth, all trying to engage her attentions at once in their agitation.

"Come with us," they said, "we can take you to this one."

"How far?" asked Lily eagerly.

"Not long away," came the answer. She knew by now to expect a journey of at least a few hours. Forgetting her fatigue and how much she had wanted to rest up, she quickly gathered her portmanteau, making sure in her excitement, to put in tobacco and tea along with the captain's bundle of letters. Admonishing Ngobi to look after both her belongings and Shiwezi, she went along through the forest with a long line of guides and 'picnickers.'

They made their way down well established paths, now forking to the left, now to the right so that Lily began to wonder at the labyrinthine quest they were on, and wishing she had a ball of string or at least some white pebbles to drop as the push of people surged on and she with it. All the while her heart raced. Was she really ready to meet Miss Poole? What would she say after all her searching, the longing for contact, and the retraint of not getting one's hopes up?

At last they came upon a village, not much of one, hidden under the great canopy. Spying only an old, wizened Faung woman in the clearing, Lily could see the huts were of the temporary kind that people made when on the move while hunting and gathering, a place that would be left to sink back into the rich carpet of soil. No sign at all of cultivated yams, so basic to any settlement, however temporary.

Her arrival was accompanied by much hooting and leaping about. It didn't take her long to see that the youngsters were taunting the residents of this forlorn village. She had only seconds to react—wondering how on earth Miss Poole could have been reduced to this—when a woman of indeterminate age emerged from one of the shabby huts: an albino.

Cowering in the doorway, what with her colorless hair, the pink, mottled skin, she was in every other way a member of her race.

Lily looked down at her own skin, flushing with embarrassment and anger. Enraged by her own gullibility and the fact that her rag-tag group had come all this way just for the sport, she wondered at whose expense? Hers or this woman's here in deep retreat, from the sun and perhaps even an outcast of outcasts.

The taunters all around Lily had sobered up, having failed to receive any lively response from her. "You have toyed with me," she said flatly, finally believing that she had found the accurate word.

And as the old woman began her own harangue, stalking up and down, pushing the bolder youths back, Lily turned away, mentally feeling in her empty pockets for some appropriate gift while realizing she had nothing adequate. "Leave these people in peace," she said.

The return hike was subdued. Mbo would never have let her go on such a misadventure if he had been around at the start of it. Damn her limitations of the language. But of course, the mistake had been her own. If she had asked to see a 'woman of the fish,' her answer would have been quite different; instead, she had asked to see a woman with skin like her own. Ultimately she had found an outcast. Would she find that Miss Poole was one too?—if she did find her. She dreaded now that she might find her in such a sad state.

Arriving back at Chief Kizudi's village at the end of the day, demoralized and exhausted, she was glad to find Mbo waiting. From his expression she could see he was relieved and from Ngobi's downcast one, she could see there had been chastisement.

Not trusting herself now she asked him to inquire if they had seen a 'woman of the fish.' Mbo clucked over her, his haughty tone and disdain for their hosts veiled by his use of English. "This is no good, Ma. These people, they know nothing. Nothing for you. You must not hear. Tea time now."

She nodded ruefully in response, going to her hut to rest until he brought her tea.

Over the next few days as the beer fermented, Lily recovered her composure and energy, concentrating on observing village life. Only the fourth day as the beer reached its zenith, did a change in routine take place as the women of the village left their usual tasks to gather for inspection.

Delighted, Lily wrote profusely on their exchanges, the gist of the conversation, their tattoo beauty treatments. Captivated, in a contented haze of her own self-acknowledged naivete, she didn't pay much attention to what Mbo did, assuming him to be engrossed in casting lots, presumably not hocking her liquor to keep in the game.

It was towards twilight as the women anticipated a night of dancing that Lily realized she had been looking at something for some days, but had not understood what it was. As with some item one loses in an unlikely place, perhaps camouflaged because the object is in a peculiar position and therefore unrecognizable, every day she had been looking at something intimately familiar. And when she realized the truth of her recognition, her heart skipped.

The chief's co-wife was wearing an ornate necklace of beads, shells, bones and feathers, each piece undoubtedly of great significance and history. Central to the decoration was a piece of what looked like bark, or lichen, or was it an intricate webbing of discolored, brown bone? Only when the wife happened to sit next to her, did Lily reach out on impulse to feel the object.

It was a piece of lace! A rose—deftly made, much like Audrey might pattern one piece after another in the evenings beside the hearth.

At first she assumed the lace must have come from her corset; there was no other possibility! Except that she knew perfectly well Audrey did not make rose motifs for her but lily-of-the-valley. Perhaps she had simply never paid attention to what lace was used on the bodice. But how could it have become so discolored already?

Had Nelson and Brodwick Ltd. traded with lace in these parts? Not exactly your usual item. Almost breathlessly, Lily left the brewery and ran in search of Mbo, calling him from a circle of men with an urgency that brought him to quick attention. Yes, he must have thought there was a crisis with his precious beer. Peta, Topi and Ngobi followed him at a quick pace. With swift strides, Lily led them back to where the women sat, defying the separation of the sexes during

72

the beer brewing.

"Ask her, ask her where she got *that.*" Lily wasted no time in pointing out the co-wife who sat looking up in astonishment.

Mbo moved forward gingerly.

"She has a piece of lace on her necklace! Ask her where she got it," Lily urged in English, lifting her own skirt to reveal the simple strand of lace that decorated her pantaloons, and in her excitement, pulled loose. Tugging it off, she gave it to Mbo. "It's lace Mbo. Don't you see? White women make it. Did she get it from a white woman like me? It could be the woman I'm looking for. Please, ask her."

Mbo took in her agitated words then turned dubiously to the co-wife and began a lengthy explanation.

Oh, don't bloody well placate her. Just ask her—Lily was beside herself. Come on, come on.

The co-wife replied amid a chorus of other voices and gesticulations. Lily could make out the sign for tumbling water, in this case, surely a reference to the Robolo. Finally, he turned to her full-face, his eyes flashing with the answer she wanted to hear. "'How come' there is a woman of the fish, Ma," he said, meaning 'perhaps.' "They have heard a story of this. These people, they have seen not seen her but the brother of this woman took his daughter to marry a man of the Robolo people, and came back with this as as part of the payment to her family. It is still many days from here to go."

Lily clutched the co-wife in an awkwardly reverent hug, forgetting completely how to keep her European sensibilities at bay. Tears glistened uncontrollably in her eyes. "Tell her thank you. Thank you."

Overwrought, Lily ran for her hut to be as alone as possible. She sobbed into her grass mat in a release of emotion she hadn't realized ran so deep. It was as though some mirage above hot, dusty soil was what she had been looking for all along—the real water at last. And just out of reach.

Margery Poole existed.

## 9.

She would find Margery Poole now. She was certain, as certain as she had ever been about reaching the fringed coast of Africa. It was simply a matter of some days and transport.

And here she was, stuck in the middle of a beer celebration, expected not only to be sociable, but available as the honored guest. It was almost unbearable.

At the center of the village arena, men had carried the huge pot of beer and placed it ceremoniously on a hot bed of coals which remained fed by the women as needed, so keeping the lumpy mixture frothy. From this pot, calabashes full of the refreshment were passed around, supplemented with shots of whiskey from Lily's stock, the bottles eyed as ultimate prizes.

Lily took a ceremonious sip of the stuff, rolling it around her tongue before she swallowed, careful to keep from screwing up her face at the sharp after-taste. She had not been able to distinguish the finer differences of these good brews—they all tasted equally foul to her. Taking her cue from Mbo who seemed very pleased with himself, the situation and the brew, she courteously bowed to Shiwezi, giving her the respect and honor not usually meted out to under-wives. But Lily wanted all to see what a prize of a wife she had along, and besides, Shiwezi had proved herself beyond a doubt.

So, it was not a great surprise for her to see that somehow, Shiwezi had received the bit of lace Lily had torn off in a wild moment—tiny tatted lily-of-the-valleys in white against the dark copper skin of her breast bone.

All was as it should be. Except...

...Except that Lily was restless, and there was no way to rush things. She had not felt such an urgency since Audrey helped her catch the boat. Then it had been understandable, the culmination of months of planning, years of reading. How could she explain her edginess now, this new consuming purpose?

She watched the dancing grow wilder through the night, the men and women becoming more openly flirtatious as the great caldron of brew emptied, and the drum beats magnified. By the time a late moon rose, Lily was at the point of taking nips from a bottle of scotch herself, strengthened by the great energy, the giddiness of the dancers stamping, the men and women singing back and forth to each other in courtship. Was it possible for hundreds of bare feet to shake the earth so? Or was it the drums, the rattles, hands against hides, soles against soil—all of it as one.

As she took another furtive swallow of liquor in the darkness, flames from torches lighting up the swirl of dancers, she remembered the evenings at home when her brother, Edward, would play the clavichord in the parlor as she brought in a tray of coffee for him. Such doleful tunes. No, she didn't mind if she never spent another evening like that, even if it did mean no mosquitoes. Her mother had liked his playing, found it 'soothing to her nerves;' meanwhile Lily had fought back the screams clinging silently in the back of her throat so that she had never finished her own coffee.

Feeling her throat, she could sense the drums vibrating. And up and down her own body. If she wanted to scream now it was out of desire for the same kind of abandon and release as the flirtatious dancers let loose against each other. She knew she did not understand their codes, nor share their knowledge of sensuality, but she had her own. She knew her own, unnamed as it was. She knew the unmistakable throbbing of life. And the hunger for it.

The morning brought a profound lull in the village. Nobody moved, either in their huts or in the open where some had decided to lie down and sleep.

Lily groaned on her bed of packs. At least no one was peering at her anymore—the novelty had worn off enough. There was no hope of pulling her escort into action. The beer stupor would have to run its own course. She knew she wasn't going anywhere till Mbo presented himself, tidied up—skin oiled, hair gleaming, his long lashes drooping a bit, in what Lily only knew to call sheepish. I hope Mbo didn't go to sleep with the wrong wife of the wrong someone. Please, she begged silently, let me get out of here before some brawl ensues, especially with Ngobi. May he hold his liquor. There was nothing to do but wait it out, they in their fog, she in her own.

While waiting all those days for the beer to brew, she had spent time sitting under a tree looking at the river which sped towards the Robolo. Would she go by canoe down those rapids? She had never seen a canoe that capsized but it certainly happened. It could easily be her canoe, even though everyone would appease the river before pushing off with her. Somehow these rapids were more ferocious than what she had experienced on the Upper Oguye. The Robolo was not known to be a quiet river; how clever of Miss Poole to move up into its inhospitable reaches. Who'd want to come this far to find her?

At last, when it was time to get her journey underway, she understood through Mbo's translated discussions with the chief that following the tumbling and reckless river would put her too far downstream from her destination, and that her route lay through forest trails once again. She was also well-versed enough to know that walking meant a hunting party would certainly go with them, and that Mbo would be much more interested in such a diversion than to get going with the expedition. How could she ever forget that transport in Africa was an event, with its own rules and pace, palavers and preparations beyond her control?

Leaving Chief Kizudi's village amid songs of farewell, Lily and her party set out into the forest. Hunters from the village went with them to hunt for meat which would be seared and smoked over spits, and then portioned out. At that point Lily and her party could take leave, and continue on their own.

76

In her impatience, she did not want this custom, and felt her failure as a leader, wondering what kind of fuming and puffing Fitzi-patricki would do in similar circumstance. Oh, but she was forgetting something—the hunt would be right up his alley. Somehow, even though she took the time to make sure her pistol was clean and in good order, it was hardly comparable to the fire-arms Fitzi-patricki might take along. Well then, she had no gentleman's club back in London to report back to.

Instead, while Mbo and all the men went off to hunt, there she was sitting among the great tree-buttresses with her field notes at base camp again, foraging with Shiwezi, measuring massive tree-perimeters, making sketches on some new kind of compound leaf, and recording folk stories she had heard. Before, this role had never bothered her; usually her feet were sore enough, and she was glad to sit with a cup of freshly brewed tea. Besides, how could she melt into the foliage the way they did on silent feet? What would it be like to have only her skin between herself and the elements, feeling every leafy branch?

Also, she had no idea or reason to think that the village hunters' quarry was different on this occasion. Nor did she care much until she was sitting there in camp, pen poised in mid-sentence, disconcerted by an eerie hush that descended over the forest. Glancing up from her papers, she noticed that Shiwezi was uneasy too, pulling Mtoli from the ground up to her waist, her head tilted, listening.

And then the sound came like an explosion, only distant. It was a great wail, no, more like a scream of anguish. Who could make a cry like that? The sound was followed by blood-curdling whoops and wild shouts. Shiwezi ran over to her, crying out urgently, pushing Lily back against a tree. What the...? Lily gasped, looking about, expecting some great tree to come crashing down upon her. There stood Shiwezi protectively, smack in front of her like one of Audrey's fierce brood-hens with feathers bristling, wings outstretched and facing outwards against danger. Lily's scalp bristled in fear; she would not have bothered to worry except for Shiwezi's action which amazed her, and made her feel how ultimately vulnerable she was. Now what? Lily's hand moved slowly to the revolver in her sash. Somehow she didn't think a shot or two would save her skin. Bloody hell, she thought, I'm going to die—*damnation*—I'm sorry, Audrey, and I was just about to find Miss P!

Within moments, a shrieking, shouting hunting party danced back into camp, feet pounding the earth in fast rhythms. The usual jubilant hunting success-song was missing. She had never witnessed a war chant yet, but she guessed that she saw one now, though could not fathom why. And brandished there, high on top of an upheld spear she saw a head set on a pike. Was Fitzpatrick's intimations of cannibalism correct?

No, she didn't have the stomach for this spectacle, even though she stood solidly on her feet, legs quaking beneath her skirt.

It was an ancient looking black head, deep crinkles across wide nostrils, large teeth bared. Gritting her own teeth as she peered over Shiwezi's shoulder, she realized it was not human but some sort of ape.

Her mind thinking back quickly over all her mental notes, she remembered Fitzpatrick seeing great apes leaping through the trees. He said they slept in nests high off the ground. Had they really killed a gorilla? Was that what they had brought? But why?

A loathing rose up into her throat like bile. She had grown used to the skinning and cutting of carcasses for food, had steeled herself to understand and accept that fact of life and death, but this was something different. Steadying herself, she stepped forward to confirm her understanding by inspecting the prize that the dancers were obviously presenting to her. Unrolling a mat out on the ground, they placed two large hairy hands and feet with elongated fingers on it. All the while Shiwezi sang out something, perhaps revulsion, certainly some kind of pained horror, or diatribe, not budging from Lily's side.

"Mbo," Lily called tersely as he loped towards her. "What is happening? This is not meat we can eat. Tell Chief Kizudi that I am glad his hunt was successful but I am not sure at all that this can help us on our journey."

To herself she swore because she was visibly unnerved. Turning away to gather up her papers, she could not stand that the hands looked so human.

Mbo scrambled to followed. "I cannot tell him this thing. Bad thing. An insult. He pays you great honor now. We must thank him, Ma, or he must find something else for your journey, and this is not a good thing."

She paused. Human and non-human sacrifice was as old as time. People killed their enemies and displayed them in grisly ways for far more brutal hungers. There were executions simply to end bids for power.

"Heads will roll," she muttered angrily in English, shaking her papers as she stowed them in her portmanteau.

"Mm?" Mbo still hovered about her, and the tempo of the dancers had slowed way down. All the while Shiwezi strutted, clucking loudly, baby Mtoli watching from her back with his wide eyes. Finally, Mbo turned to her and said something. Shiwezi became quiet but not without giving him a withering look.

"Why is she upset?" Lily touched his arm for reassurance.

He nodded his head dismissingly. "She afraid for you."

"Indeed...?" She rallied. Whatever Shiwezi's actions truly meant, Lily could make out a show of loyalty when she saw one. As 'co-wives' they had a give and take established that she took to heart."Do we have meat at all?"

"Oh yes very, Ma." Mbo brightened, whistled for Peta who held up a large buck, already skinned.

She swallowed hard. "Then all is well. Carry on. But on my journey, we must hunt only for meat. Wrap up the head, the hands and the feet for the Chief. He has hosted us well."

Mbo was displeased but he did not spit. "You give him too much. This is not a good thing...."

Why? Because he doesn't want to be in debt to me? Or do I become in debt to him? *I don't know what this all means!* She yelled inwardly, pacing and fuming in frustration. Is it an issue of pride and power here? Why is Shiwezi still so upset? What is she shielding me from? Will I be killed if I don't accept? Why do I feel as though my life hangs in the balance?

"Very well." She nodded. "Let us take his trophy." It would be simple enough to bury the gorilla remains along the way somewhere, after they had parted from the chief.

Mbo turned back to the gathering, satisfied, and Lily went to nurse a worsening head-ache, her ears still splitting from the sound of that soul-wrenching cry, the war-cries, and Shiwezi's echoing wail. That wail, yes, too much like the wails back at the Franch Mission....

Margery Poole may well have escaped the clutches of European society, but what had she found instead? Life simply became something else, molded by the unknown which sprang from a set of rules she didn't understand. As with the language, she didn't know where to begin deciphering idiom from the literal. She looked forward to speaking English with someone, and yet she wondered if now she *could* say anything that wasn't mixed up with new words and sounds.

But yes, she did yearn to understand the implications of such critical moments.

All night her head throbbed, the pain splitting the back of her head, so that she had to sit up with her head resting on the skirt pulled taut between her knees. And all the while Shiwezi slept close beside her, baby Mtoli between them. Lily felt as though they were intrisically bound together now, for better or worse, and vowed to hold up her end of the unspoken bargain.

In the morning she still hadn't shaken the pain. It was the worst head-ache she could remember, pushing her beyond endurance. Unable to eat, she took to plodding along the path, numbly in her place with the others, and then only because she had no desire to sit in one spot any longer. She couldn't even hold down her tea. From time to time she stopped, throwing up, more like excessive and dramatic spitting. They must think I am absolutely disgusted, she thought ruefully, keeping one eye closed as she stumbled. Head-aches from the sun or due to fatigue were one thing; she had always been able to shake them. None of the others seemed worse for the wear. At one point, it was Shiwezi who stopped the party; indicating to for Lily to sit down, she took to rubbing Lily's temples with her finger-tips, even crushing some leaves she picked so that Lily's skin prickled from the oils. How delicate, yet firm Shiwezi's touch was. After that, Lily was able to drink some tea and keep it.

Only the next day did Lily began to feel the haze of pain lifting, tense as she still felt because of Chief Kizudi's presence. Shiwezi remained close to her the entire time.

How have I made it at all, Lily marvelled, all this slogging through bog and forest from one river simply to find another? Then at last she reached the Robolo itself, not the deep chasms she had expected, but a part where the dark green water ran relatively smoothly in a navigable stream, even sporting a few crocodiles here and there.

When her party finally reached a fork in the river where two branches of the Robolo met, Chief Kizudi bade them a positively jolly farewell, providing a roasted bush pig on a black, sandy bank, before fading off into the forest with his retinue at last. So what the hell was all that about the gorilla?

Relieved, Lily stood a long time on that bank, its sandy grains left over from some time-forgotten volcano, pondering which direction to take as she sucked the last rich juices from a pork rib. The southern branch of the river flowed west with calm resolution, while the north fork frothed over sharp rocks at the last moment, fighting to join a smoother current. If I wanted to cut myself off from the approach of whites, thought Lily, that's the way I'd go.

Backtracking, they forded the wider, converged river, waist deep, at a relatively shallow spot where a sand bank jutted in, and where her escort could keep a eye on crocodiles that skulked nearby. After fording the river, Lily took the bundle of gorilla remains and threw it in the river, Mbo remaining silent where he stood, leaning on his spear while Peta clucked in disagreement. Clapping her hands in sharp strokes, as if to shake of the whole experience, Lily picked up her portmanteau. As they started off again, Shiwezi seemed more relaxed; she began to sing. They wended their way through underbush until they found a path that hugged the bank of the north fork of the Robolo River.

Lily's shoes were falling apart, rotting along the seams, and she vowed that at camp that evening, she would bind them together as best as she could. The one other pair that she still had in her belongings, had to hold out for a time when she was nearer the coast.

She was watching her feet tramping along one more arduous mile when they rounded a bend in the stream and the path, startled by the sound of scythes and excited voices. Mbo stopped in his tracks, Lily pushing up behind him to see. Shoving passed him hurriedly, she dropped her portmanteau.

Down the path, surrounded by a group of black people, just as she was, Lily saw a white woman.

The woman cocked her head in surprise, eyes squinting against the sun, disbelief surpassing her look of curiosity and deepening amazement. All this in the slight movement of her eyebrows, the slight quiver of her lips.

Lily forgot everything she was going to say, everything she had saved up or mulled over as an appropriate greeting.

"God above," said the woman suddenly in plain, honest English. "Is that an angel or just a European on my path?"

Lily stepped forward, in a trance of her own. There before her stood a small woman, her skin a tawny brown like the sleek hide of an antelope and accentuating the grayish eyes which shone like river-pebbles—not anything like Lily had ever imagined, and certainly no Aunt Vanessa. Arms bare from the shoulders down, legs showing up to her knees, she wore what looked like the scant remnant of a petticoat or night-dress, stripped of its lace. Wispy brown hair, bleached pale and coarse by the sun, hung in choppy tresses to her shoulders as though she had hacked her hair off with the blunt side of a scythe.

At first she saw this fellow European as any Englishman might have—stung by her near nakedness, wanting to tear open her packs and offer up decent clothing. Captain Lowell had been right—this woman had indeed become 'bush-crazed.' She couldn't help thinking that her worst imaginings about Miss P had been realized, that she was indeed living in neglect like the albino. Then her African gaze came into focus, sharp and self-reprimanding; the woman who stood before her was alert, poised, bold—definitely expecting some sort of coherent greeting in return. In truth, Lily wondered if she had ever seen anyone more beautiful.

Flustered, she took off her hat and managed a polite, "Miss Poole...?"

## 10.

Miss Poole flashed a wide smile full of blunt, unfiled teeth. "I didn't think anyone would ever really bother to come up this far—at least not until someone decided to put a railroad through—but I wasn't counting on that. You must be a fool." Then, as if she had dismissed Lily's existence with these words, she turned back to her own party standing beside a gnarled, twisted tree with some quick instructions. The men who had been chopping at the side of the path began their work again. It looked as though they were hacking out a path.

What had Lily expected? Someone who would rush into her arms with floods of tears grateful at being found? Instead, she was accepted matter-of-factly as if she were a casual acquaintance who had just arrived for afternoon tea and whatever matter was at hand was to be paid attention to first.

After Miss Poole had turned away, Lily noted that besides the working men there were four or five Faung woman with Miss Poole, all in great agitation. One woman with fear in her swollen and averted eyes stood naked among them, naked in that she seemed to be stripped of any beadwork at all. Having met up with Shiwezi, Lily knew enough to guess that this young women was also an outcast, what with the obvious, bloody gashes on her arms and chest. On her head was a basket and by the cries issuing from it, seemed to contain a baby. The other woman hovered about her protectively.

"Don't mind us," Miss Poole said over her shoulder. "We have to cut a new path to my village because this woman has been branded a witch and would defile any other I have and

84

nobody would want to walk on it, much less enter my habitation. You have a choice to go up the path a bit further—if you have half a care for your mortal safety. Or you can come along if you want."

Lily didn't hesitate, but swallowed her own emotion and followed, saying, "Of course." She didn't even notice that she had left her portmanteau abandoned in the middle of the path, nor did she know that Shiwezi picked it up for her.

"I didn't see any fetishes as we came," Lily said to a background of swishing scythes against the tall grasses and weeds as they slowly cleared a path. A shout interrupted her as the men chased off a snake.

"That's right—you'd find them further along. My compound is outside of their influence," Miss Poole turned slightly as she spoke but never stopped walking. Lily noticed that she wore rudimentary sandals made out of hide, perhaps something she had fashioned herself. "Believe it or not, I have my own sphere of influence." Her face crinkled into that smile again, her eyes bright with a flash of gleeful wickedness. "For one thing, I have lamps at night. And I know how to keep a flame  from flickering. That's big magic, right there, don't you know."

By this time the path had opened up to a clearing which turned out to be a cluster of huts, all daubed in distinctive black clay, and bamboo-grass storage sheds. At first glance Lily almost thought she had entered a prosperous village of some important man, what with the clean, shady courtyard, meat drying on racks over smoking fires, and most evident of all, a large number of women at various tasks. A palaver of men, squatting under a boya tree some distance away was ignored by the children who ran about everywhere, naked, brown and full of squeals and laughter.

It was the general feeling of the place which she found remarkable and different. For one thing all the women stopped what they were doing which was unusual, and turned with easy smiles, gentle, musical greetings, some coming forward to Miss Poole who stretched out her hands to each in turn.

She spoke some swift sentences in Faung, so that Lily could barely catch the meaning. Some of the women in the courtyard brought out mats to sit on, while others brought linens, or the remnants thereof—grey but clean, and a basin of water. They began to wash the woman's wounds. It was then that Lily felt another presence, turned to meet the direct, appraising gaze of an older woman. By her attire—layers of necklaces with fetishes and pouches of medicines she was a diviner in her own right. Meeting her gaze sent a shiver down Lily's spine, not of fear, but of an understanding; the woman had touched her across the short distance—a gentle touch, but as though her very soul had been fingered, sized up for its worth, then set down again. Set down but not discarded. Yes, Lily felt it; she turned disconcertedly away to watch other actions.

"There there now," Margery Poole was looking in the basket, then reached in to pick up an infant, gently lifting out the baby who cried fretfully. Cradling it in her arms, she smiled. "Her child has been born with a birthmark down her left side, see, and so, must be an evil sprit. We will give her to a woman with milk until we can get her mother to feed her." Only then did she look up at Lily matter-of-factly; her deep grey eyes had a fierce sparkle in them. "The mother was being chased out of the village, and would have been beaten to death, and her entrails cut out. She was a wife of Chief Zwemuweli, and to produce such a child would bring a blight upon his village. Only my diviner, Mkumi's quick presence there, saved her."

"I see," said Lily, reaching out to touch the girl's tiny fingers. How odd to see the raw white and mottled mark on the side of that small dark face.

"Yes, we'll have her among the living, won't we, little one? All my children here are outcast babies, one with a deformed hand, or else twins or one surviving twin—double births are considered evil spirits, or one of them is anyway, but which one? Both must be killed. Outcast babies, all, usually along with their outcast mothers. Which of them is evil, can you tell?" She waved an affectionate hand as she gazed at the children in their play. "I unwittingly gained considerable power just by housing all these children—to keep these many spirits at bay must prove formidable. Why, obviously, this little girl must have been bewitched by me to have such a hideous pink mark, what say you? Please have a seat on that mat, if you want. I'm sure you have been on your feet a good while...."

Lily nodded and went to sit. Mbo looked a bit bewildered as he entered the village, frowning, sensing the difference, just as she had. As Margery Poole tended to the baby, Lily, greeted him light-heartedly, and told him to make the men comfortable while she beckoned Shiwezi to join the women. Of course, Mbo would be concerned—here was a village of strong women and no chief to keep them in line.

"Take some tobacco with the pipe," Lily called after him, good-naturedly, so that his face brightened, and she caught a glimpse of his teeth. She waved an arm at him, then turned back to the shaded mat. She realized she was trembling.

"Of course we shall have tea presently," said the hostess, totally absorbed in bathing the baby and smiling into her small face, the eyes opening and shutting. The baby still whimpered. "Bush tea, of course. I only have black tea on Christmas but you came just in time, I'm almost out. You do have some, don't you." Then to the child, "Absolutely hungry, aren't you? No wonder, empty belly, and no stomach yet for milk. Birth is difficult, I know, birth is most difficult. Here...." She handed over the baby to yet another woman who to put the infant to her reluctant mother's breast, coaxing it to nurse while Miss Poole cradled the head and looked on with approval. She and the woman began to laugh happily as the baby responded, and the mother's eyes seemed to shine even through the fear.

"There now," Margery Poole turned her full attention upon Lily with a clap of her hands, her palms staying together. "I'm all yours for a moment. Tell me everything. How was your trip? Lord, we haven't even been introduced though I take it you know exactly who I am."

"Yes." Lily flushed, trying to hold her own gaze steady in answer. "My name is Lily Bascombe and I came to Africa to trade. Captain Lowell was the one who asked me to find you, if possible."

"Well, I should hope it wasn't easy. I haven't been particularly eager to be found. I have not even seen a trader for many years since I came to this place. Of course I was always expecting some red-faced, puffing man in a pith helmet pushing his way through the undergrowth. That just didn't make much sense to me—who'd go to that kind of trouble? I didn't dream it would be a woman." The way she said 'woman' was hushed, even apologetic in tone.

"No, you didn't make it easy," countered Lily, smiling now that she could reflect on her voyage. "And perhaps I wouldn't have found you—but that's a story in and of itself."

"I'm sure." Margery Poole fetched a tin mug from a low wall, and a woman brought over a small three-legged pot of steaming liquid, while another brought a cracked tea cup trimmed with flowers but no saucer. Surely that china cup had been carefully guarded, preserved by Miss Poole, a fragile connection with her past. Dipping in the mug and portioning some into the cup, Margery Poole then passed the pot on to the women who were gathering about on the mats, keeping shy company. "I will introduce you to everyone in time, but I think for the moment I shall practice my English. Here, have some tea. Be careful, that cup is the last I have."

"Thank you," said Lily accepting the china cup reverently, wondering if it was too early to present the tins of tea and tobacco, but she hadn't unpacked them. She didn't know what to say, where to begin; she was just so relieved to be where she was that she sagged, overcome. She wanted to hug this woman out of sheer joy as though she had come home. If she trembled, she hoped it wasn't obvious.

"You will want a hut I suppose, and will stay a while. You're not hurriedly on your way somewhere else, are you?" Miss Poole seemed to be scrutinizing her, in much the same way as she had sized up the situation of the babies moments earlier.

"No, no. Eventually, when my trade goods are gone, I am to make my way down the Robolo and meet a steamer at the coast. I would very much like to stay a bit, if it's no trouble."

"Huts are put up in a day. Meanwhile, please stay in mine with me. It is quite spacious and comfortable. I see you have

brought a woman along. Very sensible of you. She is lovely—
and the baby. Which man is her husband then, that tall lis-
som scout of yours?"

"No, no, we found her along the way. She is in my guardi-
anship—I took her on as 'second-wife' with promises that it
was all right with my husband. I married myself quickly by
proxy to Nelson and Brodwick Ltd. to assure her." Lily
laughed nervously.

"Which one of them?"

"I made no distinction!"

"Fair enough—Nelson is a bloated, half-daft lout who for-
gets his liquor is for trade. I haven't seen him in years,
thank-goodness, and alas, Brodwick died of the fever, I believe. But then, so have I. As for your wife there, you have
brought her to the right place. All the others are outcasts
too, that I have made wives. Only my husband is a spirit in
the sky. This is quite impressive to them, you understand,
for me to be wife to such a powerful thing as a spirit—
especially one associated with thunder storms. It was Mkumi's idea, anyway—she was just here a minute ago—you will
meet her presently," Miss Poole looked about at slowly the
dispersing villagers.

"I think I already have, in a way," said Lily quietly.

"Ah. Well she is the one to speak with. It is because of her
that I am here in any shape or form, and she was the one
who said I had to provide some sort of explanation for my absent husband. Anyway, I have done quite well by Him." She
nodded as she sipped her tea, went on, almost urgently. "The
people here like the Jehovah idea of God—powerful, right-
eous, forbidding like the ancestors they worship, but when I
tell them that in His Wisdom and Love, He is the Light, they
say that even at mid-day, there is a pool of shadow at your
feet, ready to spring out again. And I say, yes, but the Light
is very strong and keeps the shadow very small and insignificant. They are in turn, skeptical, because shadow must inevitably return—night is complete shadow when all the dangers are loose. I say, you must keep the Light with you
always, indeed that the Light will stay—even a little is
enough because it is full of Love. But love as we define it in

all it meanings, does not begin to have the same meaning here. There are barriers at the very root of our concepts. I say it is an absence of fear, but we are still discussing all this." Miss Poole sat down on one of the vacated mats, sipping her tea, talking avidly as though she had been saving her thoughts for a long time, and now they bubbled out. "I have never imagined sitting like this explaining such things to anyone. But then I have never imagined a woman coming here." It was as though she were taking a deep drink, or else testing to see what Lily's response would be.

Lily proceeded thoughtfully. "What you say—that's quite different from the iron-clad and imposed method on the mission stations, is it not? I imagine the Mission Board has not taken kindly to your interpretations out here."

Margery Poole scoffed. "What do they know? They make assumptions, that I toe the line—I don't bother trying to define what I do. Oh, how can you convey a message if the basic concept is not only foreign but completely baffling, no common point of reference? Besides, as you know, I have essentially broken away."

"They apparently still see you as part of them, at least by the letters I have brought," Lily answered quickly.

"Of course, because I am a white woman off in the bush, and they are responsible for me. I only get away with it because Africa presents highly unusual circumstances. They can't cast me out—unlike these women here—and the friend you have brought with you. You may think you have saved a soul, but there are dozens like her. They get discarded in domestic quarrels among the wives. The next village picks them up as slaves, and then the old village raids to scoop them back, dowries used up long ago."

"Shiwezi was on her way home when we found her—living on her own. I changed her status. Any dowry will have to be given to me."

Miss Poole went on testily, "So you think you have improved her status? No matter whom you give her to, you won't be around to insure the dowry is kept honorable. Surely you must have noticed her posture towards you when you took her on. Hm? As soon as your back is turned homeward, her husband will take away her marriage skirt for some other arrangement. It is her mother's brother who must look out for her, protect the honor. Wars are fought over this, curses cast, appeasements sought. The women are chattel. It is outright slavery."

"I find that hard to believe," said Lily vehemently. "Mbo's tribe holds their women in high regard."

"And so do we back in England, my dear, within the tribe, as long as the bride price is right and fortunes don't fall. Honor, yes? Where do you run from a failed marriage—to Africa?"

Lily sat perturbed for a moment, looking at the thick leaves in the bottom her her cup. "You are bitter."

Margery Poole laughed, a hoarseness to her voice. "Bitter? I simply face facts. I have lived here for a time. Did you, then?"

"Did I—run away from a marriage? No. I was attending my invalid mother until she died."

"Aha, and you want to talk to me about slavery?"

Lily recoiled. "I did it out of duty!"

Margery Poole called over her shoulder for more tea, turned back, her eyes twinkling. "How well we English disguise it. Duty, yes. They fool themselves here too."

Lily turned the tables, snapped. "While you, I suppose, are free? Aren't you out here due to some spiritual or moral duty?"

"A higher calling?" Her eyes crinkled in genuine mirth. "That's what I like—a good argument. And in English too! I'm quite surprised I can even converse, though I do try and practice by talking to myself. You too? And as for me, the reasons for my being here have changed over and over. It began by my father being a clergyman. I was raised to become a missionary, you see, consecrated for the task at my christening. I think it was my father's only claim to an act of imagination—his daughter would be provided for, and trained to serve where he himself could not go due to poor health, you understand. He did this with my younger brother also. My younger sister was spared only because she was lined up to take care of my parents in their old age. My brother never got off the boat when he sailed here towards the equator. He went into soldiering and liquor—where did he go?...Southern Africa I think. I have no idea whether he still survives, probably not."

"What did you do?" Lily asked respectfully.

Miss Poole's tone became slow and measured. "And I, well, I had to wait until I got onto a mission station. From there it was bit by bit. It became evident almost as soon as I put ashore that the native people had more to teach me about life than I had for them. I volunteered for the outposts. About all I had with me was a Bible, a hymnal, and a rudimentary medical kit. From there it was God and me on my own—mostly me."

"But you have been back to England!"

"No, I didn't get out of my furlough, did I? Oh, I suppose I had to go take another look as what I was leaving behind. They expected I might find a reasonable suitor for marriage back in England and lead some quaint pastoral life, be safe and provided for, half daft as I was...Even I thought...oh, that there might be some other path for me." Miss Poole shrugged, as if resolving the past with a pause. "But here I am—my own mistress. What rules I don't observe are of my choice. To the Faung I'm odd no matter what I do. Independent woman diviners are rare among these tribes, but like Mkumi, there are some. And so they have a healthy respect for my brand of witchcraft."

Before Lily had a chance to ask more, Margery Poole rose, washing her mug in the basin of water and with slow, deliberate movements, placed the mug on the low wall. Lily stood up hurriedly, following her example. She was totally taken by her host's manner and tone of voice, abrasive as it was, wanting to remember everything that they had just said.

"You can settle in now. I must see to the babies."

"Babies?"

"Oh, we have more than one, my dear. Lilly followed her into a hut. Margery Poole led the way by ducking through doorway hung with frayed gauze into a large, circular hut with its dark and cool interior. "Actually have a real bed, until the termites finish it up." True enough, there next to a simple wash-stand was a wide bedstead of bamboo, lashed together and with an obvious sway to it. A mattress of hay was covered with a simple blanket, and hung about with a generous amount of mosquito netting. Margery Poole had known what to bring with her, ultimately. "You may have it— I am quite used to sleeping on a mat."

"So am I by now," Lily objected. "Or else I use my packs."

"A good way to keep track of them, I'll warrant. Choose what will make you comfortable. I'm off to the children now. You will find me easily."

"Yes, quite." Lily watched her go out and across the courtyard, not wanting to settle in at all, but to go along. Somehow, she felt instantly dismissed, practical as it was.

## 11.

After bringing packs into the hut and arranging them as she had by habit for a long time, she eyed the bed, then stealthily strode over to try it out, more importantly to pull the netting all around and sink back in the luxury of a place away from the relentless mosquitoes. The china cup was one thing, but to find that Miss Poole had kept this one obvious object of her civilization seemed basic, now that Lily had travelled. She simply had not foreseen the brutal reality of insects, and dismissed mosquito netting along with such things as Fitzi-patriki's tent, canvas bath-tub or silverware. But his tent had surely included one, and in her denial, she had made a mistake. Surely, this was heaven; she couldn't even hear them in her ears. And if the mattress was slightly lumpy, it was smooth compare to the lumps and bumps of her bundles. The bedstead itself was more sturdy than it looked, just crooked.

Her head was still spinning from the aftermath of her headache and she still shivered with the excitement of find-ing Miss Poole at last. Was it truly possible? All due to a piece of lace on a necklace. She couldn't believe that she might have slipped out of that village without the people bothering to discuss the fact of another white woman. How easy it would have been to slip away, disgruntled over meet-ing an albino.

But if no one had ever really seen Miss Poole, maybe they would have assumed she was one and the same. Perhaps that is why they so readily greeted her....

She sank back, meaning to rise up and see what her hostess was doing, but fell deeply asleep instead, more deeply than she had in months.

When she opened her eyes, blinking, and disoriented, it was to a voice calling gently through the netting to her. Turning her head, she could see a figure in white next to her, a dark toddler riding on the woman's hip.

"Ndoshi—my 'sunshine on the river'—and I came to see if you were ready to keep company," said Margery Poole. "He is quite surprised to see there is another woman like me, and so are they all. Your coming has caused quite a stir. Two women who travel without husbands?—This is truly remarkable."

Lily sat up heavily, chilled from her sleep, and yet her eyes were still burning. "I wish I had had the foresight to bring mosquito netting with me. I have just had a sleep of sanity."

"Oh, it's a must if I want to outwit the fever. However, I am philosophical enough about it to know I can't," said Margery Poole as she walked outside. "We have food prepared."

Rubbing herself to wake up, Lily went to her packs and pulled out the tins she wanted to present, and from her portmanteau, the bundle of letters which had been the reason for her quest. As she stepped into the courtyard, the setting sun bathed her in warmth, casting a rosy glow across the sky, the dense forest all around taking on a golden tint as the greens deepened, the shadows lengthened. But her eyes sought out Margery Poole who had set down the little boy, squatted low, taking a wooden bowl of food in her free hand to feed him with the other. She looked up at Lily's approach, her eyebrows rising and falling in a quick gesture of acknowledgement. "Ah, here comes my 'Visitation.' Are you really made of flesh or are you an apparition, some trick of the Light?"

"Something you have inadvertently conjured with you own powers? No, I can guarantee you I slogged my way through all kinds of situations to arrive here. And I am very much flesh—the discomfort I enjoy due to insect bites can prove that." Lily held out the tins. "Look, I have brought you something. If you can grasp them, surely you will know that I am not some sort of mirage."

Margery Poole laughed, an open-throated chuckle, and took the items. "Not at all. Spirits are known to seem very real and even give tokens that are very solid. What have we here? Ah, it must be Christmas—tea, from England, it would appear. What's this?—tobacco! Good God, matches too? Do you know how long it has been? Captain Lowell did send you after me then, didn't he? He is a good man."

"Yes, he told me you enjoyed tobacco. He gave me these— including a letter of introduction—and I must confess, the proposal set my goal quite differently at that moment from my rather undefined intentions before."

Margery Poole looked up into her eyes, almost quizzically, perhaps taken aback, as she reached for the neatly tied bundle of letters. "To bring me these?" She shook her head sharply. "You shouldn't have, no, not for these."

The rebuff stung Lily, so that she stepped back quivering, as though all that she had endured in good faith to come so far, had no meaning. She had never questioned whether Miss Poole would want the letters or not.

"But isn't there news from your family?"

"My family is here."

"And I believe the Mission has sent you your salary."

Margery Poole glanced at one of the envelopes, tore the end open, examined the contents. "A voucher saying that my money is being held for me in Newtown. Good Lord, what is this?" She pulled out some ten-pound notes, gave a short, shrill laugh as she let the notes flutter to the ground.

Lily moved quickly to retrieve them. "This is to pay your passage."

"Passage? I'm not going anywhere I would need that. It is useless to me here."

"But what about when you go home?"

Margery Poole rose slowly and went to sit on the low, mud-daubed wall, looking weary all of a sudden. "To England? Nonsense. I don't intend to."

"Perhaps not now, but what if you change your mind?"

"This is my life now. There is nothing in England for me. What a ridiculous idea. I'd die there of either consumption or constriction."

"If you stay here, you'll die of fever!" Lily's tone was adamant, at the same time she was aware that she was pleading, and didn't quite know why.

"Ah, I'd much rather die of fever."

"You are impossible!" But Lily said so playfully, taking a seat next to her host. Her head was beginning to throb again, her emotions in a jumble.

"Yes. But you are the first to say so in English. I was always very compliant before, and very quiet about things. Oh, I knew my mind, but I was waiting. In this life, I have the chance to speak my mind as much as I like. I have the sense that we are alike in this regard."

Lily nodded, because in fact, she felt quite speechless, keenly aware that she knew what it meant to bide one's time and hold one's tongue.

She mustered her courage, the very thing that had driven her onward to begin with. "I came to Africa to trade commodities, establish a route, if possible. It did not occur to me that you would not wish to communicate with the world outside, because, after all, you know about it."

"Yes, well as I have said, I had always dreaded the day of my 'discovery', but I had expected a man. Silly of me.... I would have told him off, found it necessary to remove myself even further. But that it should be a woman, this is quite another matter. Do you shoot big game?"

Once again Lily was caught off guard. "Why, no. No. Mbo and the others hunt for me when we need it. I do carry a pistol. I had, I had to shoot a leopard...."

Margery Poole tilted her head, a glance at the fast disappearing sun. "Well then, perhaps you are not here to bag me as a trophy, if you see what I mean." With that she rose to fetch more food from the pots simmering over the coals.

"Of course not, of course not!" Lily sprang up, a despair clutching at her heart. "I came...I came to trade experiences, if you will."

"Here is a bowl." Margery Poole handed one to her. "I trust you are used to eating with your fingers. Experiences, ah—what I have to show you is as simple as this bowl of food here...." She stopped as if in mid-thought.

"Yes, and I have a place that I love—shall I take you there when you are fully rested? Would you like that?"

"Very much."

As darkness fell and the tree frogs, the crickets took up their choruses, the villagers began to light lamps, based on the ancient biblical model, a wick dipped into clarified fat within a clay container. The flames that did not flicker belonged to three large lamps set beneath the glass funnels from safari lamps. Margery Poole lit these lamps, one at the doorway of her hut and two within.

"Surely you can't rely on a supply of whale-oil," Lily asked, enjoying the steady glow. "And venison doesn't supply fat...."

"Hippo is in plentiful supply."

In contrast to the flames of a camp fire for months as the only source of light at night, something she was well used to, looking around at the sea of lamps, Lily felt bathed, one circle of light receding into the strength of the next. She wanted to stay awake and talk long into the night, but she felt hollow with the strain of her long journey, spent. Why so tired, now that she had found this safe haven and someone to really talk to? How come her very limbs seemed to be on fire? Why did the lamp light blur in her vision?

If she had hopes of immediate adventures, her body set her on another course.

*　*　*

How many days and nights did she lie on Miss Poole's bed tossing in delirium? At one point she thought she was drowning in a vast, deep swamp and cried for help, but Mbo and the others were off hunting. Off hunting. Off hunting. Or she was in danger, looking up into the tawny eyes of a leopard above her in a tree. A leopard flicking its tail, ready to spring, and her voice caught in her throat with terror.

Every now and again, she could hear Audrey in the kitchen while she lay on the bench by the stove. Why was Audrey using her for a laundry rack, hanging dripping towels on her that were meant for her sick mother? She tried to stop her, flailing to push the wet, cold cloth away, only to be held down firmly. She could hear a voice talking to her in English, calm soothing words like a lullaby, but it was a stranger's voice, not Audrey's. And there were women standing all about her. They smelled of musk and sweat; their hands rubbed her legs and arms with tingling oils that reeked. And always, Audrey's towels upon her which she tried to remove because they were steaming—she was too close to the stove and the towels were getting too hot. Someone would open her mouth and she would bite down on a wet cloth, and the taste was bitter but cold.

Then she would sleep, a deep but ragged sleep in which her head was splitting open. And if she stirred it was because her mother was ringing a bell upstairs, summoning her. Would the bell never stop ringing? Why couldn't she rise up to answer it?

She would awaken to Audrey putting those towels on her again, or the bitter rag in her mouth, but this time she didn't care. She felt hands upon her, a woman talking to her. At first she strained to make out the language, to translate the words, but then she realized she was hearing a tongue she knew already. English! She could feel the woman next to her, either sitting or lying close by, but it wasn't Shiwezi, because there was no baby rustling between them or climbing over her. The woman would call to her, "Lily Bascombe," or sometimes just "Lily." She heard her say, accusingly, "If you are an angel, you can't go about dying on me, now can you? Of course not."

Those last words made a deep impression. Of couse I cannot die, Lily thought. I must find my portmanteau. Where did I leave it? And she did not fight away the damp towels anymore.

She woke up suddenly one time, clear-headed but her vision glazed, and found an extraordinary woman, unusual because of her cropped hair, gazing down at her with beaming grey eyes. The woman was rubbing a damp towel up and down Lily's bare arm which she held up, then dipping the towel into a pot, wringing it out before rubbing her leg next. Lily was aware that her clothes had been taken off. "I believe you are coming around," the woman said. "Do you know who I am and where you are?"

"Yes," Lily cried hoarsely, but it was as though she could

not find her voice. "Yes, I have been looking...I have been looking for...you."

"And you found me. Just in time by the looks of it. Here now, you must drink some of this. Dear Miss Bascombe, you came to me riddled with fever."

"Did I? I'm sorry."

The woman touched her cheek tenderly. "Don't be silly...."

And then Lily sank away again.

# 12.

"You were in delirium for four days and nights," Miss Poole said, handing Lily the china cup full of a strange-smelling brew.

With one of her shirts wrapped around her shoulders, but otherwise only in her undergarments, Lily sat in the afteroon sun on the low wall drinking as she was told to. She smiled weakly, "What am I drinking?"

"Something Mkumi has taught me to make from various roots. It is to bring out the fever poisons, and rebuild your strength. How you made it to my village!—I'm beginning to think it quite miraculous. Weren't you warned about malaria?"

"Not sufficiently," Lily answered weakly, thinking back to Louis Gilbert who had hovered on his bed for six days with fever before dying.

"If I have one consolation it's that malaria will keep Europeans from coming into Africa. Even that, I suppose, will not hold back our kind."

"No, I suppose not."

"I was concerned that we could not break the fever, and you fought us so! How you flailed about. Shiwezi came to help, you know, and Mkumi. We rubbed your body with oil up and down to cool you off and calm you down, and Mkumi sat outside my hut dispelling the evil she had drawn off from your body."

Lily was startled. "How did she do that?"

"You think I jest, don't you?"

"Not at all," said Lily, offended.

When Miss Poole saw that Lily would take her seriously,

she described how her diviner had rubbed Lily from the head down, flinging the evil out of the soles of her feet and into a small bowl, then taking the bowl off into the night to chant over it, ridding the pot of its foul spirits which had to go back into the forest where they belonged. After all, the mosquitoes were merely the messengers of these more ominous shades.

"Am I better now?" asked Lily.

"For the time being, but you must be careful as you now have a predisposition, like I do. You learn to live with it. You must rest some more days until you have your strength back."

"Yes, you were going to take me somewhere."

"Soon," Miss Poole nodded warmly, patting Lily on the thigh. "When you have your strength."

The after-glow of that touch lingered long after Miss Poole had marched off to her various tasks—a touch already deeply familiar. That touch had kept her alive.

For the next few days Lily spent her time walking about the village, the children curiously following her or presenting her with flowers, a toad and other small forest creatures which she sketched in her book. She watched the women make clay pots out in the sunny courtyard, followed them to the river where they bathed the children or dug up black clay from a generous deposit. And near the village, she helped Miss Poole carry stones to make a small pond where a spring gushed out of the earth.

Finally, she was deemed strong enough to consider an excursion. At dawn the next day, the air was cool. Thin layers of mist hovered over the river which Lily could see from the open courtyard in front of Margery Poole's hut. She stood with the cracked china cup full of steaming black tea. Her hostess took her own tin mug between her hands, and sniffed the steam deeply. "This will take us to the top of the mountain," she said.

"A mountain?"

"Oh yes, my mountain. That's why you had to be strong. It's a hill really. You can't see it from here because of the forest rising away from the river. But you shall see it presently.

Thunder storms tend to gather about it and rattle around. As you might guess, this is beneficial to me. That I am on friendly terms with the top lends credence to my position here. I go up every so often. I suppose these excursions could be termed as my conjugal visits!" Margery Poole laughed a wide open laugh, head thrown back.

Hurriedly, Lily turned away to fill her cup with more tea from the pot, but she was blushing at Miss Poole's frankness, and furious that she felt awkward at all.. After a moment, she turned back, recovered. "When do you wish to depart then. What provisions do we take. Should I ask for just Mbo to come with us?"

"I have food arranged which we can carry ourselves, and no, as a rule, I never take anyone with me. I know the way—the game trails are quite clear, and beyond that to the summit, I have established a path with a panga. I do take a scythe, a panga. Take your revolver if you wish but I don't think you need to. I don't have one and have survived quite sufficiently." With that Margery Poole settled back to her tea, offering Lily some meal 'cakes' that had been cooking in the coals. Once the soot encrusted outer layer was removed, the warm mush on the inside, sweetened with wild honey, was a pleasant surprise. Lily ate voraciously, anticipating the climb ahead.

After her host had discussed various matters with her companions, and Lily had assured Mbo that she would be fine, the two Europeans finally left the village, but not before Miss Poole had brought out a pair of rudimentary shoes for Lily who looked down at her own sorry versions, and was quite happy to change. The new shoes with their hide soles fit like supple slippers once she had tied them on with the sinew laces across the arch of her foot. There was a great deal of commentary and laughter among the villagers, standing about bare-footed as she tried them on. True enough, tying a wad of leather around one's foot must have seemed ridiculous. Her one consolation was that her feet were comfortable.

The sun rose, promising its full, eventual heat as the mist on the waters evaporated, and animal life on the river shift-

103

ed. As she walked along the path of tall grasses, Lily caught glimpses of heron, done with their fishing, taking flight, while on rocks out in the current, crocodiles began to stir in the sunshine and slip into the water.

Before long Margery Poole led them away from the river into the forest, and Lily could feel that they were beginning a slow ascent.

Miss Poole walked ahead carrying a hide satchel of food over one shoulder, and a gourd of water on her hip. In her right hand she brandished a scythe which she swiped with here and there, clipping vines or brambles out of the way. Lily followed, matching the efficient pace, carrying only her skin of water and her pistol in her sash. But she was aware that her comparatively cumbersome clothes must be more of a burden than the weight that Miss Poole carried.

How she wished she had the courage to go bare-legged; she could see the knotted muscles of her companion's calves below the ragged hem-line. She had walked plenty of times behind the Faung and admired their physical beauty, but to discover that a European woman had legs of such muscular beauty was a shock. She had the recollection, like a half-forgotten dream, of a woman's red-booted calves—but she had never ever dared imagine Aunt Vanessa having strong bare legs! Why not?

But what she liked best about this 'bush-crazed' woman was her lack of self-consciousness, as though that had long been discarded with her shoes and her pantaloons. When had she discarded her corset? Why, this woman was almost as free in her body as the Faung. The only difference was that bounce to each step, while the Faung could practically glide wherever they went.

The climb proceeded without incident, no great cats or snakes lurking about, just the requisite monkeys, birds and lizards. Conversation remained at a minimum, except for comments about particular plants or trees. Margery Poole seemed absorbed in her own thoughts, and so Lily let her be, satisfied with Margery's low humming—some Faung rhythms: bmm-bmm zeh-um bmm. Lily did not know enough Faung to join in, yet for the life of her she could not recall an

104

English country tune.

They made their way up through a bamboo forest, the bamboo thick as trees but without the undergrowth. Here came a blue-green stillness, no monkeys chattering or leaping about in the canopy. Some of the bamboo stood as thick and tall as columns like a ancient palace with a sound like the sea whispering above their heads.

"We are almost there," said Margery Poole in a hushed voice, her grey eyes alight. "It is like some lost, forgotten city perched on the hillside, with great boulders that attract the lightning, hung about with vines like the gardens of Babylon gone wild." She laughed then. "Like me."

Her description of the place was true enough; the bamboo forest grew thinner, lighter, until the two women found themselves crossing a reddish grey ledge of rock covered with lichens of every color. Great spires of rocks stuck at all angles, some steep and impossible to climb, others offering ledges and footholds. Sure-footed, Miss Poole bounded up along a recognized route while Lily scrambled along after, overcome with heat and a heaviness in her limbs. Pin-pricks of pain went up and down her neck and she hoped not to have a recurrence of her terrible head-ache, not here, not now. She was blooming-well happy and didn't want the day spoiled in anyway.

At last she found her host seated upon a large flat rock, scythe having clattered to one side, hugging her knees in a loose, languid pose while gazing out. Lily stopped to catch her breath and look at what Miss Poole gestured to with a sweep of an arm.

"Here is the Land of Milk and Honey. All of Africa to the east, Miss Bascombe!—the only such view that I have seen. Sometimes I can detect a large area of blue against the horizon, some large lake I suppose, but I like to pretend it's the ocean." With that she opened the satchel and pulled out a clay pipe which she filled slowly, deliberately from the tin of tobacco Lily had brought her. "There are creatures out there who have never seen people and have no need to whatsoever."

"It's wonderful," said Lily, fumbling to sit down as she took in the hazy vista of rolling green hills, a faraway, winding river and great smoky mountains at a vast distance. "Fitzpatrick thought to mount an expedition and find the source of the Nile, somewhere beyond those mountains."

Miss Poole laughed. "Wrong coast for Lake Victoria! Has that been established as fact now?"

"Yes, but the maps I have consulted have no real accuracy yet as to distance from this coast. A great deal is still only estimation. I think it would be quite something to chart it!"

"You would have to find the continental divide because that river there flows north but empties into the Atlantic just like the Oguye, if I had to wager on it."

Contented with such a simple, realistic response, Lily let go of something then, something that had loomed in her mind—a question, an aspiration—since the day long ago upon Aunt Vanessa's knee. For, in essence, she was looking upon the source of the Nile, the 'unexplored forests of equatorial Africa' where rivers began, and she was satisfied. She said, "This is what I came to see. A woman in my childhood planted the idea. She was going to find the source of the Nile. It was what made me dream—to come here."

"Ah, we may as well all be seeking the fountain of youth! Or die finding it! I was wondering why you chose to come to this part of Africa— She didn't tell you to come find me, did she?"

Lily laughed, "No. I came this way because of Fitzpatrick, to see for myself, perhaps make further contributions. And I thought if I came out this far, I might see a way to go further the next time. In a sense this was to be my trial run, create some kind of foothold."

"I suppose you have found that then—in my village." Her host waved a hand to the east. "Yours for the conquering!"

Lily gasped, "I don't want to!" before realizing the sardonic tone of that statement.

A pair of twinkling eyes seemed to appraise her, and find her fit. "I came here one Easter, camped out all night to see the sun come up. Light a match for me, will you, so I can cup my hands to keep the wind out." Miss Poole handed Lily the matches, and Lily carefully complied until the pipe glowed in response to vigorous puffs. "Delightful. It has been

106

forever. I was sure I had relinquished the habit. I have even tried to make pipes to no avail—Let's see, oh, I don't know if it was Easter exactly but the sunrise was spectacular. I felt as if I were the first person to see the day."

Lily nodded in response. "I could almost feel like a poet up here."

"Ah! Tell me, what would the poem be like?" Miss Poole blew smoke from the corners of her mouth.

"Alas, I am not a poet, the strong images are right in front of me, but I have no words to make out of them. It's just a feeling, the romantic in me, I suppose."

"And not the mystic, nor the spiritual?"

"I'm afraid I'm not well-versed enough to claim that," Lily stammered, wishing she hadn't said anything.

"Come now, it all has to do with a kind of passion, does it not, pure and simple, the passion of feeling connected...." Miss Poole stopped in mid-sentence, pulled the pipe from her lips to point out a kite. The bird reeled in widening spirals below them. "I have always come here alone, you know, never thought I'd share it with someone of the same language, similar sensibilities, much less to find I would share it with someone of my own kind, a woman. You have come as a great surprise to me, you know." Miss Poole grinned, clenching the pipe between her teeth.

Heady and overcome, perhaps by the thwarted poet within, or perhaps by the wide panorama stretching into lonely reaches far beyond them, Lily blurted, "Africa has made you beautiful, Miss Poole."

"Oh," She scoffed, her eyes crinkling up in amusement. "It must be some illusion. You are seeing something familiar, a reflection of some kind—another white woman! Something you can understand in a place where you are otherwise, always a stranger."

"No. No," said Lily sharply. "I am talking simply about you, that you are beautiful."

"I am burned by the sun, my brain shrivelled like a raisin. I am scrawny and wizened, and most certainly have no decent clothes. Hardly an exemplary specimen of my race! No, you are mad. Beauty is down at the coast where the colonial women keep their skin milky white under their parasols." Margery Poole's words came fast and furiously, her disclaimer like a taunt.

"I have never—I never thought...." Lily stopped at a loss. What did she mean? Suddenly, she was overcome by the shyness she had felt earlier. How could she express it—that she had to come all the way to Africa to find the kindred spirit she had always hungered for? A friend—oh yes, she knew Margery Poole was a friend. Her heart ached. Joy made it ache so.

Gently, Margery Poole laid a hand, gnarled and muscular, on Lily's knee, fingering the white cotton of her skirt. "You are a romantic, my dear. The very fact that you searched for me, tells me so, and then to fling youself upon my doorstep in a high fever....!"

"I didn't fling...." Lily stammered, recoiling inwardly, vulnerable. She realized that this woman already knew her body, was familiar with it the way any nurse is, indeed, the way she was with her mother's physical demands. Yet this was different.

Miss Poole went on, "It becomes you. I thought I was a mystic all this time, myself. Perhaps I am not, after all." And she sighed then, but did not move her hand while Lily braced herself against the hard rock because she was trembling as Margery Poole continued, "There isn't much room for our kind of romance in Africa, as such, Miss Bascombe. What with the parasites, the disease, the daily potential for disaster. The Faung do not have the concept.

"I find here a people who are straight-forward in a way that we no longer know how to be. The way the men of the tribes exchange women and wives attests to that, but also, their fights, their wars—all have very basic, sensible provocations like a debt to be settled."

Lily pondered that observation, keen to share her own. "Perhaps it is that I find no artifice here. We Europeans have become quite good at facade, have we not, the art of deceit? Class trappings and all."

"Interesting. Or is it that you have yet to delve into the cunning of the African shadow-world?" Miss Poole tapped with a finger on her lower lip. "Yes, I will give you an example. When I was a child, and my father donned his clerical robes, it was to remove himself from the congregation, becoming holy in a veiled way. Here, one doesn't separate out the spiritual. A dancer donning a mask, is in fact, making the spritual realm terrifyingly present—something to be dealt with. They make no distinction between the spirit world and this one. It is all real, entwined, influencing thought and action both ways. What we would call madness is their ecstatic experience of the reality of that spirit world. Even our language is inadaquate. Living with them, I wonder where we got some of our notions. Or if they have similar notions, I can't recognize the form at all.

"What's more is that I think we Europeans are very foolish to try and come into Africa and make a great to-do over what we call divine love, as though one can simply love by conviction. For love of God, their faith is in the power of ancestors whom they must honor. Why do they need to substitute the the power of our white man's God. You can talk about good and evil, you can talk about loyalty and even honor, but love....? I do not know how to begin defining that...." Miss Poole broke off, apparently at some sort of loss, reached for the water gourd at her waist and opened it. Putting aside the pipe, she offered a drink. Then abruptly, "Please, do call me Margery."

Lily smiled unabashedly as she took a sip, her eyes meeting Margery's across the brim of the gourd. "Thank you. Yes. Call me Lily."

"Like 'Llile in Faung, the sorceress—I like that. No wonder I take you for an apparition."

"Like all of that?" Lily flung an arm out towards the view.

"What I look at out there, and what I sit on here is all very real and full of spirit—life force—yes, even these very rocks we sit on," Margery went on earnestly. "This is understandable. The people here tell me life is in everything. Spirit is in everything. Yet, there is a fatalistic element in how this spirit is manifest, but what is it? While we Europeans believe in our own sort of external superlative—Is it God? I think about this a great deal, but perhaps we can reach some conclusions together."

"Is that what you wonder about up here?" Lily gave back the gourd and stretched out against the rock to look up at the sky with its hazy wisps of cloud.

"Oh, earlier I used to bring my Bible up here and read portions I liked, but my Bible disappeared some years ago. It was bound in black leather with gold-leaf trim on the pages. A beautiful book, my grandmother's—she gave it to me when I first came out here. Somebody obviously thought it was a significant fetish. Now, I suppose I consider what I do up here as meditation, posing too many questions. But my mind is a maze—I always come up against dead-ends, or questions. I end up in a deep silence—sometimes I'm happy with that, sometimes I feel entrapped."

"And what will it be today?"

"Something quite different—a pleasant distraction?"

"Mmm mm." Lily responded, unaware that she had picked up the Faung manner. She proceeded ruefully. "I'm thinking, about how even their good spirits have a penchant for trickery, however benign. I have witnessed this myself. I lost my corset to the river spirit and it turned up downstream in the form of a mask on a dancer's head!"

"You had a corset?" Margery slapped the rock in astonished mirth. "Here in Africa?"

"Yes." Lily jumped, stammered, "I—I know that must seem odd to you. And I'm not saying that the river spirit didn't do me a great favor. Do stop laughing...."

But Margery was lying flat out on the rock, holding her stomach and laughing, tears in her eyes while Lily waited it out in embarrassment, reminded of an earlier event when she had seen Mbo and the others rollicking on the ground with laughter. She tried to rally. "I mean, what I was trying to say is that if a corset looks like a mask to the Faung— which it did, I have to say it made a great deal of sense. What I'm getting at is form, how and what we recognize or don't. If something is totally out of our experience, how do we recognize it? In the case of the corset-mask, a benign spirit was at play. But what about when the form represents danger? When all we can do is fear it simply because it is foreign and we don't know how to interpret it?"

"Ah, ah!" Margery sat up slowly, coughing her laughter away, sputtering, "You have a point, you do have a point." She touched Lily on the shoulder with her finger-tips. "You must pardon me but I haven't heard anything so funny for a long time. And it's only because I left my own corsets stuck under my pillow the night I packed for Africa! Odd, how we get rid of things, isn't it? But then, I could get away with it because I have always been scrawny, really, and I am quite flat chested."

"You are?" Lily said too quickly.

"Don't you worry, when you get back to the coast, those milky white ladies will have you fixed up in no time. They will try, mark my words." Margery clucked, looking Lily over. "But what shall we do about those freckles? I do declare, we can only hope they will fade away on the passage home."

Lily clutched at her yellowed clothes, her rolled up sleeves. Of course, she was already unpresentable. Somehow the gesture meant more—she didn't want to give up her freckles.

"Come now, let's have something to eat," said Margery, opening up the satchel. "What about nice egg-salad sand-wiches, cold kidney pie? A crusty, buttered roll?"

She pulled out wild plums, strips of smoked meat and a starchy squash which had been baked in its hard shell.

"I wonder," Lily said as she accepted a portion of the food, "what has become of your Bible?"

Margery snorted, looking up pointedly, "As I said—odd how we get rid of things, isn't it?"

## 13.

Making their way down the mountain was as happy as the ascent but with a sense of achievement.

This mood was interrupted suddenly by urgent voices calling to Margery, long before the path met up with the river.

"Something has happened," Margery said turning to Lily. "Come, we must hurry." And she called, sing-song, in return.

So, here was Margery being summoned again. Lily felt a rush of anticipation, quickening her pace.

They soon met up with five women from the village, all in a great state of agitation. Mkumi, the diviner, led them; she was the elder of the village, senior in age to Margery, and carried the social stature of a 'co-wife' in Faung terms. Lily had learned from Margery that she was a fast friend, a partner in a scheme greatly different from anything heard of in those parts, or perhaps anywhere. A vital link to the surrounding villages, Mkumi helped Margery with the interpretations of customs in all their intricacies, all their subtle changes depending on the situation.

She spoke loudly, adamantly, the others a chorus of agreement and comment, but so rapidly that Lily was lost. It hadn't taken Lily too long to realize that even though these people were Faung, they spoke quite their own dialect. Despairing, Lily wondered how she was ever going to understand or be understood from place to place.

Margery turned to Lily. "We have been raided," she said, matter-of-factly, her eyes no longer bemused.

"Tell me?" Lily asked, breathless.

"We have always been well prepared for such an event. It

is an inevitability, tit for tat, but I haven't ever actually been raided before. So, of course it's unprecedented. Unfortunately, circumstances have changed, and I never could have foreseen this. I should have when you arrived."

"Why?" Lily pressed, beginning to feel uncomfortable.

"Because it is Shiwezi whom they have taken."

"Shiwezi?" Lily drew up. "Who, how?"

"The village of Chief Zwemuweli. Undoubtedly, news has travelled of her beauty. That man who has been lolling about—his brother too and an uncle of one of the other women we took in—oh, they come and go like spies. With you out of the way he took the chance. He has been in debt, you understand to the chief. With you out of the way, there was no clear protector, and my own companions were in an unknown predicament. Who was to answer for Shiwezi? Her son certainly isn't of age."

"What do you mean? Who has to answer for her?"

"A brother, an uncle, a son. But just bringing up their names is enough clout. There is a whole taunt that goes on, you see. The raiding party, usually five or six men, in paint and masks, and with spears too—they come in and 'shake the women up' verbally. The woman must defend themselves or their co-wives and concubines with exclamations of their lineage—how they are immune." Margery's explanation tumbled out as they hurried home. "Sometimes the men are very brazen, and sweep a concubine off—perhaps one whose relation has a debt or is considered too cowardly. And so, no one answered for Shiwezi. She was an easy pick."

"Where was Mbo then?"

"Right there, undoubtedly enjoying the theater of it all." Margery turned; her mouth slanted sardonically. "Why should he answer for her? He is not a relation, nor are any of the other men."

"Well, he shall have to answer to me!" Lily shouted, enraged.

Birds shrieked above her in response.

"Don't shout," Margery answered in a hushed tone. "Don't get angry, yet. That is a sign of cowardice so soon. And you can't blame Mbo."

113

"He is in my employ," Lily argued tersely, her voice low and urgent. "She is my co-wife, and he is supposed to be helping me in matters."

"Oh, you can wish that all you want. It isn't the way it works, Lily."

Lily started at the sound of her name; her voice caught. "Not one of my men did anything?"

"What, and escalate the problem? Really, you must understand, they didn't have any right to interfere."

"That's unacceptable! Then I must go after her myself."

Margery stopped her, putting out an open hand, fingers pressing against Lily's chest. "Why? Is it for love?"

Lily was silenced in her fierceness, stopped cold in her passion. What did that mean—for love. It made her feel ashamed and defensive. She stood by me, she thought, during the incident of the gorilla. When I was down with the fever, she stood by me. Now it is my turn to stand by her. "They know she is my co-wife. I must answer for her."

"Ah, is it a matter valuable property then? Is that why you want her back? Because she makes a high quality beer?"

"I want to get her back because I took her on. I took responsibility for her. She is with me."

"Honor then?" Margery had not yet withdrawn her hand, but her other hand now played along her own cheek as she scrutinized Lily's face.

"Loyalty, if you will. Is that what you meant when you said love?" asked Lily, evenly. "I care about her."

"You care about one individual among hundreds like her? Why?"

Lily began to panic, irritated. Was this a continuation of their conversation on the mountain? Was she being accused of European sentimentality? She said rather defensively, "Yes, she makes an incredible beer. It makes us more presentable to new tribes." But the panic still washed over her like it had in the forest that time Shiwezi flew in front of her, hands outspread, arms flailing up and down, warning her, caring....

"Yes, she is useful." Margery withdrew her hand.

"Damn."

114

"Gracious, do you swear too? Mbo probably boasted about her qualities, don't you know?"

"Boasted, when he wouldn't even answer for her." Lily brandished her revolver, checking the bullet chamber.

"My God, what do you think you're doing?"

"It's my fetish, isn't it?" She aimed it at a large lizard sitting on a rock with its beady eyes, its pulsing throat.

"Oh darling yes," chided Margery, "do let's take home its head and mount it in your game room."

Lily flinched, her lips pulled tight across her teeth, her nostrils open, but she pointed the gun above the trees, and fired.

A great shot split the sky, ricocheting through the canopy. Lily's body shook with the rebound. She lowered the smoking barrel with its left-over stink. And as she had known, a loud cry from the disturbed monkeys rent the air.

Down the path, the women turned back, screaming alarm. What had been struck by lightning in the middle of a clear day?

"Hm," Margery stood with her hands over her ears. "That was quite powerful. I'm sure this forest has never heard a sound like that before, but will undoubtedly again. Did you find it satisfactory?"

"Yes. Yes, I do." Lily stuck the revolver back in her sash which she tightened.

"Good, because what do you propose as a follow up?"

"I don't know. I shall think of something. I don't suppose you have a suggestion?"

Margery began to walk again. "Why don't we declare war, two European women and a revolver against the Faung with their years—hundreds of years—of perfected custom?"

"Very well," said Lily, really peeved now. "You have made your point. I only meant it as a way of talking. That was for Mbo, he has heard it once before. I certainly don't intend to overuse the effect."

"Ah yes, when you shot the leopard. I know all about it."

"What do you know?" Lily was caught off-guard again.

"I know the whole story!" Margery gave a half-laugh. "They acted it out while you were sleeping. Very entertaining!

115

You should have seen how 'Pta characterized you. Indeed, you must have still been wearing your corset! But sure enough, with your arm up stiff as a board, you put a hole through a leopard's skull. Pity—I think they will be half-expecting you to bring home a leopard. Unfortunate that you didn't shoot the lizard. A hole through its skull would have been impressive enough."

"The lizard wasn't killing one of my men." Lily retorted.

Margery waved a hand in the air, not turning around again. "But of course."

"How would you advise me to proceed, then, Margery?"

The path opened onto views of the river. Margery stopped so that they could walk together as the path widened. She linked elbows with Lily, bent her head to speak in confidence. "I can tell you what I know of the customs, what are possible avenues of action."

"Thank you." Lily said stiffly. "That will be greatly appreciated."

# 14.

All seemed as usual as Lily entered the village, no sign of disruption or struggle. Then she saw that all the women were huddled in the courtyard with the children in a somber silence. Her party of four men were standing under the palaver tree looking like contrite schoolboys who had still enjoyed the sport of their infraction, but now came to bear the punishment. She walked up to Mbo whose lids were lowered, his lashes hanging heavy.

"I am very disappointed in you," she said crossly while looking the others up and down as well. "I am the one who is paying you, am I not?"

"Yes, Ma."

"And I give you tobacco, and I let you hunt as much as you like as we go. But you did not keep my wife here for me."

Mbo shrugged dolefully. The others shuffled.

"You should have answered for her if only on her brewing of beer! ...something you enjoyed full well yourself."

There was a slight smile on his lips but he controlled himself.

She turned on her heel and stalked back to the courtyard where Margery had taken a seat and some toddlers onto her lap as she spoke to the others.

"Was Shiwezi taken forcibly? Did she put up a fight?" Lily asked, her voice tense.

"Oh no, she went quite compliantly. They are very fatalistic about these things. She didn't put up a struggle when you found her, did she?"

"No, but she is such a determined young woman. I see Mtoli is here. They took her without her baby?"

"If the baby had been with her, he would have gone. He must have been with someone else, or perhaps she passed him onto someone when the raiders arrived. Women often suckle each others babies—they are not possessive or private about the breasts."

"I see." Lily gulped. She had never ever heard anyone talk so openly, so matter-of-factly as Margery, and so she could dare the next question. "They won't ... he, the chief, won't ... touch her will he?"

"You mean have his way with her sexually? He can do anything he wants, but perhaps not quite yet. It depends on whether he sees her as a real conquest or is she a bargaining chip? He may wait for some sort of reaction. Indeed, he has certainly heard your gun shot. I don't know what he'll make of that. It also depends how long it takes to resolve this matter, or if it can be."

"If it can? Let's have some tea. I need to think, and I need tea for that."

"Tea? Again today? This must be the second day of Christmas!" Margery called after her as Lily went to find the pot of hot water on the fire. Margery may not have had the luxury of black tea often but she had a plentiful supply of boiling water for one of her many kinds of bush tea.

Spent, Lily went through the motions of making tea as the rest of the village settled into preparations for the evening meal amid heated conversation. Her head was pounding. Surely, she was not going to have one of those headaches again but it felt as though one were coming on. It was as though the shot's kickback still ricocheted throughout her. Bringing back two steaming cups, she hoped the tea would help.

"You may as well get some rest," said Margery with one long appraising look at her. "It is going to take awhile to make arrangements with the other side of the river. I will confer with Mkumi this evening, and perhaps we can meet with Chief Zwem tomorrow. And black tea is not the thing you need—you need a tonic. No matter how much you brace yourself, you are not going to get used to fever headaches. There are ways to alleviate fever symptoms. I will teach you

118

how to take care of them. You certainly won't be of any use in the next few days if you are tossing on my bed in a delirium, eh? I shall brew you an herbal remedy and send you to bed."

Lily nodded wearily.

*     *     *

When Lily woke up in the morning from a drugged sleep but without a headache, she discovered that Margery had either retired late and risen early, or not gone to bed at all.

Slowly, heavily, Lily pushed herself off bamboo bed and stretched out the stiffness she was used to now. It was laundry day, time to take care of all the basics again. But then she remembered that Shiwezi had been taken off, and she sat down with a feeling of dread across her scalp.

That Margery had said, "Is it for love?" rankled Lily. "You care about one individual among hundreds like her?" Lily set aside that thought quickly and reflected back on how Shiwezi had come along so simply with her party. Wouldn't she adapt in a similar way to her new circumstances? Perhaps it was wrong of Lily to interfere. How did she know what Shiwezi wanted? Was she different now that she had seen another way of living? Or did she still feel cursed? Lily shook her head. How did Shiwezi see any of it?

Stumbling out of the dark hut into the dazzling morning sun, Lily went in search of tea. The courtyard was empty but she could hear the rhythmic thumps of someone grinding grain. A few children sat about in the dirt. All of the village had taken on a subdued aspect, quite different from the singing and lively banter she had heard only yesterday morning.

She knew even when up on the mountain with Margery, that she had wanted to savor every minute, take that feeling of joy with her and keep it like a smooth river stone, something to hold, take out and feel again. It was as though she had dropped the stone by accident on the way home. Perhaps why she wanted to bring Shiwezi back was to put everything in order, perhaps find that stone again. In that case, Margery would find her motivation quite selfish.

"Ah, there she is. My Lily in full bloom this morning." A

119

voice rang out clearly, and with its usual, playful teasing.

"I never quite know whether you're insulting me." Lily smiled reluctantly, turned to find Margery coming from another part of the village.

"It's simply because I'm constantly surprised to see you. If you were male and wore a pith helmet, I'm sure I'd be much more subdued. Proper, anyway. You will want your tea now, I suppose. I trust your headache left you." Margery went over to the fire to prepare a pot.

Lily followed. "Where have you been?"

"Out back in the women's compound."

"I thought this was a women's compound."

"Oh yes, most certainly, but this is the public meeting place, the equivalent to the parlor, really. Where I have been is the kitchen, the place where the women really talk and no man in his right mind does anything but poke his head in for a few minutes. But of course, here he can't poke his head in at all—literally on pain of death. We went there so we could take care of business. Lord, the women could foment rebellion out of these compounds. Perhaps some day they will."

"Perhaps we will too, we Englishwomen," said Lily with great conviction.

Margery shot her an odd look while she squatted by the fire. "Indeed."

Lily stood above her, hands on hips. "You know, you are still a subject of the Crown, even if you do see yourself as an expatriate. You could be doing the same kind of work at home. You yourself say we are still in bondage there. Why here?"

"Because it is my God-forsaken destiny," retorted Margery acidly. "I must remind myself once again that you are but a Visitation. I had best not forget that, had I? You are the one who will go back and foment rebellion, aren't you? God knows we English have treated our own kind with brutish cruelty, and there is a great deal to set right. But meanwhile our task is to retrieve Shiwezi, is it not?"

Lily shifted her weight from one foot to the other. "Absolutely."

"Good. Tea?" Margery jumped up with the pot of tea in

her outstretched hand. "Now, where are the cups? The children are always taking them. There!" She looked surprised to see them right on the low shelf where Lily had always seen them placed. "Now Lily," she said, pouring the tea. "Mkumi, who is a cousin of the chief through her mother, and one of the other women here, 'Mgamelele, also related, are on their way to the village to visit Shiwezi. They come and go often from there, so it will not be unusual, but they will state that their business is to make sure Shiwezi is well treated, and that I have been insulted, that you, as my guest, have been badly treated. They will announce that I—you and I, that is—wish to have a palaver with Chief Zwem. Meanwhile, they will convey Shiwezi to the women's compound on the pretext of wanting to examine her. In this sort of situation, as when a young girl is given out as a 'test-bride' the family can come to inspect her condition physically and spiritually. We will claim this right, or at least try for making a tattoo which is common. If you could spare some lace somehow, that could come in handy. As you can see I negotiated mine away a long time ago."

"Yes, how unfortunate that I never saw it as a trade item. I shall certainly know next time, but as long as the supply lasts off my own clothes, you're welcome to it."

Lily sat on the low wall, sipping tea as Margery continued to speak, her own mug clenched between her hands. "Then, much like the bad king puts a maiden in the castle tower, we will keep Shiwezi in the compound, except in this case, away from the bad king—until negotiation has been settled. Mkumi, at least, will have to stay there with her constantly, but 'Mgamelele will be able to come and go. The point is to get the other women on our side too—that's where the lace may come in handy. Shiwezi is an obvious bone of contention among them, but there is nothing better than taking on the husband all together, eh?"

"So, he will have her in his village but she'll be inaccessible. What about Mtoli, can we take him to her?"

"Not a good idea yet, though we will talk to her about it. She is probably already nursing a child there so that her breasts won't hurt. Mkumi comes from a line of witchdoctors, so she is a great asset to have on our side, I must say. She commands a certain respect, if not fear, so Shiwezi is in good hands."

Lily finished her tea with a growing impatience. "When do we get started?"

"Oh, they have already gone. But I have no idea whether any of it will work. You have to remember that for Shiwezi to stay in the women's compound for any length of time, defies taboo. Who wants to stay in an accursed place very long? It takes extraordinary will-power and spiritual stamina."

"I didn't know that. In Mbo's village, it seemed like such a marvelous place. I came and went from it all the time."

"Ah, well, you're an Englishwoman." Margery spoke with a quick wave of her hand, her tea mug still clasped in the other. "I must go to the children. You can come too, you know."

What a impossible person. Lily shook her head. Is she telling me that I'm an ignoramus or immune. She protested glumly, "I don't know anything about children, only invalids."

"Suit yourself. It's going to be a long wait if you sit around. Play with the children and you won't be waiting at all."

But Lily decided to catch up with her notes first. The events of the day before were going to take time to sift through. Could she even remember what they spoke about on the mountain. How could she capture the exquisite feeling again with its hope, its freedom, a wildness to the peace, when the memory of it was bittersweet?

Sitting on the low wall in the shade of a ranga tree which dropped its soft, sheathed nuts with sudden plops around her, she was reminded of falling apples as she opened her book, readied her ink and pen. Glancing in the direction of the palaver tree she saw Mbo and the others casting lots. They didn't need her permission to go hunt, but they waited for it, and in her mood, she was not about to give them the pleasure.

Now if she could only get the date right. Fetching herself another cup of tea, she smiled. Of course, it was the third day of Christmas.

## 15.

After some hours, 'Mgamelele returned, calling news even before she entered the village.

A palaver was on with Chief Zwem.

Lily knew she shouldn't have been surprised to turn and find Mbo right at her side, bumping into her. Close by stood the other three, Peta, Ngobi and Topi, ready for action, their eyes gleaming, their bodies taut. She smiled wanly at Mbo, not sure of his motives in it all except curiosity. His eyes creased in a friendly smile, his lips parted across his teeth.

This is all child's play for you, isn't it, she thought, when none of you would answer for Shiwezi. Now, I suppose that when I get her, you'll get drunk on her beer, exclaiming your heroics at conveying me there and back.

They were indeed a proud and handsome escort.

Margery seemed to have prepared herself in the meanwhile. As the party set off down the path for the river, she called blithely over to Lily who proceeded well behind her, "Didn't forget your parasol, my dear?"

For once, instead of being stupefied, Lily yelled back tipping her hat, "Yes, but I do have a revolver."

Laughter rippled over the heads of 'Mgamelele, Peta and Ngobi. Mbo, as usual, headed the party while Topi took up the rear.

News of the impending palaver had already made the rounds. The river was full of canoes cutting across the short distance from one bank to the other, all in the direction of Chief Zwem's village, all amid melodious conversation which seemed to echo in the water. And as always when there was a movement of people, the crocodiles slipped from the banks into action, their snouts, eyes, and the ridges of their backs grimly visible. Lily was always amazed that more canoes didn't topple with all the river activity. She had only seen it happen once, and everyone was pulled to safety in time. Perhaps it only served to make her feel all the more nervous.

No one else seemed perturbed. Mbo and Peta were steadying a canoe by the bank in preparation for embarkment, but Margery, who was apparently used to conveying herself, went with 'Mgamelele to secure a separate canoe, Topi and Ngobi yet another. Torn, Lily stood on the bank immobile.

"What are you waiting for?" From the bow, Margery pointed for her to climb in the dug-out, while 'Mgamelele stood in the stern, her long paddle in hand.

"Uh, so many people," said Lily, not daring to look at Mbo as she scrambled to find her balance and seat in the middle of Margery's canoe. "Why did I think this would be a quiet, private conversation?"

"Privacy? That is the trapping of those who believe they are civilized," answered Margery as she paddled. "How can you isolate yourself here when everything is connected, when everything is alive, even the hut about you. The desire for privacy is a cultural thing. Try and explain it to the Faung, and they will look at you as though you are daft. Privacy only comes out of divisions, when life is no longer communal, no longer all one."

Lily thought back to the time she had bathed by the waterfall, how even then she had not felt safely alone, yet at the same time, lonesome. She said, "What about when you go up on your mountain?"

"Ah, don't I go to meet my Maker?—or used to, until I could no longer tell what form God came in." Margery smacked a crocodile on its nose as it snooped up to the canoe. "So now I go up there for the view. That's God, I suppose, unless this old crocodile is."

The crocodile retreated at her rebuke with the paddle, but like a log it bobbed along, then suddenly sank away.

"But you have never gone there with anyone but me."

"I never said I was beyond the need or cultivation of privacy. Nor have I ever wanted to go there with anyone before."

"Oh," was all that Lily could muster.

Besides, they were nearing the opposite bank, and dark hands were reaching out to Margery, helping to pull the canoe in, but more so in greeting. She climbed out into the fray, leaving Lily to her own devises again. Lily used as much of her broken Faung as she could, making her way through a sea of hands.

Amid the crowd, they made their way to Chief Zwem's palaver tree where he already sat upon his three-legged stool, elders on either side of him leaning against the root-buttresses, relatives stationed all about on their grass mats. He wore a hat made clearly out of zebra mane from the high country. How come all kings end up looking debauched, wondered Lily, because it was hard not to notice his beer-bloated stomach, the spoiled-boy pout on his lips, his eyes yellow and heavy-lidded in the heat. It was hard to imagine him a young, supple warrior like Mbo.

Prominently squatting next to him was the witch-doctor, his face daubed with paint, switches in his hands of leopard and antelope tails. These he flicked with sharp motions to keep flies away. Or whatever else.

Margery and Lily took seats on some mats, the former squatting down and rocking on her heels, the latter, uncomfortably, with her feet tucked under.

With exceedingly slow movements Margery unfolded the bundle from her waist. The package was made of antelope hide, tied with sinew. When she opened it, and spread it out flat, she slowly arranged each object that tumbled out.

Hums and guttural clucks from the onlookers made it clear that her actions were being closely watched and acknowledged.

"What are you doing?" ask Lily in a low voice.

"I am arranging personal articles of importance. Each is a symbol of an interaction and time...."

"What are those?" Lily pointed urgently to white knuckles bones and finger joints.

"Those are from a gorilla's hands and feet. I am reminding Chief Zwem that his diseased brother was an ally of mine because he gave me the hands and feet of a gorilla."

"That's horrible." Lily shifted, straightening her back.

"Don't try and wriggle into a corset," retorted Margery. "Of course it's horrible. It's horrible when a crocodile eats a person too. The point is, we as human beings, go out and kill what we don't understand but fear. The gorilla is powerful and yet mysterious—so like us and yet not. By offering me the hands and feet of a gorilla, he was telling me at the time, that I was in essence not to be feared like the gorilla. In effect I was receiving his protection and good will."

"Bloody hell," exclaimed Lily, her head hanging as she shook it. Gorilla. Hands and feet. She remembered Shiwezi's protective anger; what had she berated the hunting party for?—that they even compared their fear of the gorilla with a fear of Lily? "What if you hadn't?"

"Why, insult him? That would be like going to dinner at a friend's and finding that you did not care for the food which your host had taken hours to prepare for you. Or worse, insinuating that it is poisoned. Why would I do that? Or at least I would have do to it tactfully. How do you tell someone politely that you suspect them of wanting to poison you? There is another dimension to it though, and that has to do with the exchange of power. By showing that I have his brother's approval, in effect, it makes Chief Zwem mildly indebted to me. This is always a good situation for me to present because it means he has to take me seriously. If I hadn't taken the gorilla hands and feet that day, I would have less to negotiate with, besides allowing myself to be feared. You enter into these balances. The point is always to show how the other is some how in debt then you can bargain." Margery spoke slowly as she finished arranging her bargaining chips. "Chief Zwem's nephew was substantially in debt to him, so the nephew's father stole Shiwezi in a raid to present to the Chief. That debt is paid unless we get Shiwezi back. Chief Zwem is perturbed because while he was immensely please to receive a concubine, he has run into trouble. They have probably already had a big family argument. That is, the nephew's father—through his sister's marriage—was foolish to raid my village. What he did was quite normal and if it had been a regular village, he would have been seen as a clever victor. The man of the village would certainly provoke war, or steal back. But by raiding our village, we have a new predicament. First of all, there is no man of the village. Also, you are my guest, and Shiwezi was yours. You had even raised her status. You have made a fuss. We are Europeans, on top of it all. See, it is impossible to know what kind of effect we have on their lives, just by showing up.

"Anyway, Chief Zwem will probably try and offer us compensation. Normally, this usually works, since he likes Shiwezi so much, and we would probably find a certain amount of antelope hides a fine trade. But we break precedent here. We are demanding Shiwezi back. We are ignoring the rules of raiding. We are co-wives, enraged co-wives, for all he knows."

"Yes, we are, yes we are enraged co-wives," exclaimed Lily vehemently, her brows knitted.

"Yes well....that may be, and this is something for him to reckon with. He isn't going to want some kind of sorcery. That's why he has the witch-doctor. I would certainly be much happier if Mkumi we here. She can rattle any mans bones. But I doubt Shiwezi would stay in the women's compound if Mkumi didn't keep her company. I will explain more as we go along. He is ready to speak now."

God, will I ever have to procure gorilla bones in front of Chief Kizudi if I want to see my waterfall again, Lily wondered ruefully, as she settled herself for the chief's long speech, and strained to catch the train of thought.

Now that the people had settled down in the sizzling heat, the buzz of commentary grown muted and sporadic, the flies came in. While Lily spent her time waving them away with her hands, wishing she had one of the witch-doctor's switches, no one else seemed to pay the least attention. Flies crawled over them, sat at the edges of their eyes. They bear up under these conditions the way I would in the dank cold back home, thought Lily shivering at the thought..

"He has finished. Did you understand?" said Margery out of the corner of her mouth.

"I'm not sure."

"He is making you an offer, just wait and see."

"But I don't want any offer."

127

"Shh, here they come."

A string of women brought beautifully carved-out gourds, some enormous. One unfurled a mat in front of Lily and the others gently laid out the gourds. Next came two men in their graceful dancing walk, carrying a large dug-out, while others followed with hides, delicate wood carvings of all manner of beasts, tightly woven water baskets, and an ornately carved wooden pillow.

"Beautiful canoe," observed Margery dryly. "Won't Mbo's eyes widen over that."

"Mmm mm," mustered Lily.

"The last goods are because he knows she is a good breeder. Quite a bargain, if I may say so myself," said Margery lightly, her eyes twinkling with that ironic amusement she took in things that Lily didn't find funny. "A handsome bride price. He is recognizing the value you place on her. In fact he is exceeding the situation, partly to make his nephew's father indebted to him for causing all the trouble. Now, even if you were a blood relation, you'd consider this proposal seriously. You would see that Shiwezi will be well provided for. How could he mistreat someone that he has paid this much for?"

"I came to fetch Shiwezi," answered Lily stubbornly.

"Yes, and for what purpose? To sell her later on, perhaps?"

"Not at all. She would have a say in where she wants to be. I don't want to be pressured into some arrangement."

"I think we need to retreat from this. It is quite appropriate and expected to meet again tomorrow. Meanwhile we can go and visit Shiwezi. You don't know, she might find this agreeable. The point is, don't forget to support their way of life in the best manner possible since we are interfering to begin with."

"All right then," snapped Lily. "Enough of the fact that I'm intrusive. I came to Africa to trade, but I had no intention of trading people."

Margery sighed in a matching exasperation. "No, there was no way to foresee that back in England, was there?"

Lily fell into a subdued silence, but nodded. She had only

wanted to make sure she wasn't another Fitzi-patriki. Even he had not traded over women. And then Margery spoke out to the chief—something long-winded and full of compliments—so that he grunted consent to a delay. All the items were removed as ceremoniously as they had been brought out.

It was time to go see Shiwezi.

## 16.

They found Shiwezi in a vacant compound except for a few women who did not emerge from their hut. She sat with her legs outstretched in the same manner Lily had seen her do the very first time.

"Tell her," said Lily to Margery as the stood before her, "that she is a proud woman now, and may greet us as one, that Chief Zwem has offered a good bride price."

Margery spoke rapidly in Faung, pulling Shiwezi to her feet. The young woman clasped Margery's hands in return, but kept her gaze down.

"What does she think of the offer?" Lily nudged Margery.

Mkumi, having stayed close by all the while began to talk to Margery who waved her hand at Lily to wait.

Finally, Margery turned to Lily apologetically. "She isn't of an opinion, what with the three of us around. How can she know? However, she seems ready to stay here, for how much longer, I can't say. She's sensible enough not to go and serve as the chief's concubine. She needs time too."

"Thank you, Mkumi, for staying with her," Lily managed directly to Mkumi who nodded, her eyes clear and serious. "With you I know she will be in good care."

Margery gripped Shiwezi's hands again, eyes telling Lily to do the same.

"Now, let's go home," said Margery briskly. "And if I may be so bold, I suggest that you make peace with Mbo. He's quite miserable."

"How do you know? Has he talked to you?" Lily asked as they bustled up the path, past fetishes, bamboo-grass gates and low branches towards the river.

"It's all in his body, my dear, all hunched, his eyes drooping. He can't possibly understand what he has done wrong, really. You must be fair with him, after all, he has travelled a long way with you. Going among other tribes has its strains."

So Lily made a point of going in his craft, and joking with him over the Chief Zwem's splendid canoe.

But even the fantasy of a wild dash down the Robolo didn't dissolve the sense of depression Lily had over the whole issue of Shiwezi. She had seen Shiwezi as defiant and courageous, trying to find her way home, to where she belonged, even at the risk of rejection which was virtually inevitable. Was it for the child? Was it an attempt to have her own childhood back. Surely she had known while she sat in her hut up on the plateau that it was all impossible. Is that why she had lingered there, living out her curse?

"Don't be so long in the face," said Margery with a raised eyebrow and her dancing eye when they reached the opposite bank. Having maneuvered her canoe to disembark first, she met Lily with an extended arm for support. "Sometimes these negotiations go on for months."

"Months?" exclaimed Lily. I don't have months, she thought. Some weeks at the most.

"Yes, these are matters that have a way of refusing to be rushed. So enjoy yourself meanwhile. You did not come to Africa to suffer except over the unavoidable things like insect bites and bouts of fever, parasites and sun-burn."

Lily didn't say anything. On the one hand, her heart raced at the idea of an extended stay, but she had a schedule to keep, a passage home arranged. It was bad enough that she lost a day or so and didn't know quite how much time she had. Could she count on the probability of her boat being behind schedule? Why languish among the colonials on the coast when she could linger here? And what if, after all the effort to reach home in time for Edward's return, he became delayed?—never mind the fact that she would lose her inheritance if she were.

They reached Margery's village in time for the evening meal, Lily writing up the day's events while her hostess went off with the children.

"Hm, pen and paper," snorted Margery, passing by Lily's elbow. "I haven't seen that in a great while." She touched a page, felt it between her fingers, sliding them over the surface. "Why do you try and set things down upon a page—does your memory fail you or is it for posterity? A published account of your adventures to make your fame and fortune? Ah, throngs of admiring people at your feet, hanging on your every word. What?—do you think you'll gain a private audience with the Queen when you get home, a seat of honor at the table? She is no greater, I daresay, certainly not nearly as astute or regal as Mkumi who walks about right in our midst without any ado. But then, I wonder if you can truly see that."

"I want to keep a record—the folk tales they tell me, my encounters...."

"Not about me, I trust. Leave me out of it," she said pointedly, and then departed without further comment.

Lily's heart sank. How could she not write about this woman? Why the hell had Captain Lowell given her those damn letters? In her burst of annoyance, her hand shot out, tipping her ink bottle. It tumbled but did not break, but a spot of dark blue liquid bubbled out onto the dun-black ground.

"My india-ink!" She cried, the sound catching in her throat. Quickly she retrieved the bottle, holding it up to the light—half gone. And her last bottle too. She would have to water it down. It would simply have to last her until she got back—of course, she had to go back. For one thing, her supplies were limited. And yes, the whole idea was to write about her adventures. Indeed, she was going to have to make a living off of it if she could. The whole point was to have a bag full of stories. She had had too many years of isolation; she wasn't going back to England to sit and rot. No longer would she be mute, 'in her place.' If anything, she wanted to blow holes through Fitzi -patriki's theories and attitudes!

Indeed, she would write, audiences with the Queen or no: *The situation over my co-wife grows more complicated, and I am now very simply bound to this place until some kind of resolution. Miss P (Here she scratched with her pen and re-*

*wrote) M is vitally helpful—ah, she saved my life—and yet, what a contrary person.*

Lighting the way into her dark hut at dusk, Margery set a small, flickering lamp down on the simple table within. Lily joined her, sitting on one of the packs that formed the end of her bed.

"I have put the children to bed. We sang together. Would you just look at this," Margery said irritably examining a tear in her dress. "I don't suppose you have thread for me to mend these tatters. I ran out long ago, and perhaps it's pointless. Why do I cling on to these vestiges of my civilization anyway—is it that I know I can never become truly native?"

Lily rummaged in her packs. "Is that the only dress you own?"

"Pretty much."

"What will you do when it wears out? Oh, here we are." Lily produced an old tea tin which contained spools of sturdy cotton thread she had brought for beading trade.

"Go about in a beaded shirt like normal citizenry around here."

Lily handed over a spool. "You know, you should really go find Nelson or Brodwick from time to time and buy some cloth with those pounds I brought you."

"That lout? Oh pardon me, your dear husband!" Margery snort was more of a hiccup. "I'd rather stay here and go around half-naked. But you will probably leave me something so I can go about 'decently,' eh? Though why my breasts should matter now, hidden or exposed, is besides the point."

Lily shook her head, saying quietly, "It's not seemly somehow."

"Pray tell? Because I'm European?"

Lily fell into a flustered silence.

Margery shrugged one shoulder at a time out of her sleeves, pulled her top down and bared her breasts. "Perhaps I should start now, a simple skirt and some beads, and refuse to acknowledge the sin of shame we have been born and bred to."

133

Lily started at Margery's action but did not move a muscle. Did she gape, even as she bit her tongue? She wanted to touch each of those deep, fleshy curves as they glistened, pale in the fragile glow of the lamp, each nipple like a pinpoint of light. She had grown used to touching everything she saw: the water, the hides of animals, leaves, bark, the skin of people, their hair, and their carved wooden fetishes. This time she made no move with her fingers, but her eyes became fixed upon two grey ones which gazed at her frankly, openly.

"And you, Lily—all buttoned up!" An arm's length away, Margery reached over and undid the top buttons of Lily's shirt. "Hm, porcelain buttons, now that would be another item for trade. I haven't seen buttons in some years—not used like this anyway—can't say where I lost the last one though I do see them crop up on necklaces. I had almost forgotten about them. It gets that way here, you see. But you, you need them still—your buttons, do you not? What with your private, if not shamefully firm and bulbous breasts." Unabashedly slipping her hand inside the shirt, she rested her palm firmly against Lily's breast. "Yes. What a shame to cover these."

Trembling, Lily did not flinch or make any effort to remove Margery's warm, vibrant hand, but slowly covered it with her own.

Margery spoke softly, "We keep too much to ourselves, covered up the way we are. Talk about being bewitched—it's part of what isolates and keeps us apart. That is why I say what I do about nakedness and touch. I have been stripped bare here of all I have ever known so that I cannot go back."

"Your hands, they touch me with such love." Lily looked into Margery's eyes which were alight, dancing with the reflection of the lamp on the table.

"Of course I do, Lily. I recognize you, perhaps only because I have lived among the women here so long. Perhaps it is because you came all the way here, and all of a sudden into my life. Oh yes, I know you were searching me out, but I had no clue, no divine sign of your coming. The form is new, you see—I didn't know it would be like this."

134

"Know what?"

"That you are my beloved."

Lily gasped, retorted as Margery had done earlier to her, "You, you only say that because I am like you!"

"Perhaps, but you turned away from death when I called you. And tell me, if a Faung woman met another Faung woman in the heart of London—would they not cleave to each other, bound very much by their common experience of finding themselves in an alien land to begin with. God forbid they would find themselves corseted! Anyhow, you are like enough to me that I may know."

"I am but an illusion, a Visitation of your own fabrication!"

"No...." Margery shook her head slowly, her voice low. "In this you are mistaken—it was none of my doing. Nevertheless, you come to me like a long-awaited lover. I didn't even know...I...."

Lily nodded hotly; she had no doubt it was all true. "Romantic or mystical?"

"Don't the two become the same? Come here to me." Margery pulled Lily close against her. They held each other a long time, breathless, suspended, cheeks touching. For Lily it was as though a shamelessly tropical sun had burst through the layers of fog that had chilled and cloaked her life, smothering her too long. And so, she certainly did not care whether they stood there in the center of the hut like that all night.

A distant rumble in the sky startled them.

"Good. Come outside with me, Lily...." Margery took her by the hand and led her out, holding her about the waist when the reached the courtyard, her chin resting on Lily's shoulder so Lily could feel those breasts against her back. "See, we are to have a storm. Now this kind of divine support I understand. It is most timely. Chief Zwem will take note of that. Now if only I could aim a bolt of lighting like you do the revolver, I could set something into motion!"

The pungent smell of rain filled the air as the sky cracked open; thunder banged and rattled overhead. Even in the darkness they could see the mass of clouds boiling over to-

135

wards them lit up by an eerie, sulphurous glow.

"Rain will keep everyone in their huts. Let's to ours then," whispered Margery. "Lie with me, Lily, will you? We will hold each other through the rain."

Lily turned her face to Margery's, their lips brushing, then stopping in one simple kiss of assent as the first drops splattered in the dust.

"Is this how Shiwezi feels in the women's compound?—a great fear, and yet a possession of power?"

"How so?"

"Aren't we defying some taboo?"

"To touch each other? Perhaps in some other ungodly place like England; not here. The women here all sleep together, sometimes in a great big heap. It is a way of life. Oh, they go to their men but it all has to do with the rains and the moon. And you, I suppose will go to your dear husband...." teased Margery, kissing Lily's collar bone, pulling open her shirt. She didn't let Lily answer, but put a finger across Lily's mouth. "Shh. Don't be affronted. There are those who don't go to a man at all, like Mkumi or her beloved 'Mgamelele, the one who has a burn scar down her side. You have to endure the stigma of being barren to do that, but it is possible. And perhaps you have."

"A way of life?" Lily whispered, frowning slightly, but Margery's hand smoothed away the crease in her brow.

"I have been the foolish one to sleep alone in my hut, to have no child at my breast. To be barren and alone. At least a barren woman has the rights of midwifery. I too am learning this skill. They know each other intimately because of childbirth, you see. They sing each other loves songs and lullabies, share the children. So they go to the men for conception, but pregnancy and the act of childbirth belongs to them only—they guard this like a treasure. Do you know it is a great secret—childbirth? The men guard their secrets of warfare, of raiding because they don't have childbirth. It is in great passion for each other that the women bear children. They dance for each other through labor, caress each other— even when there is no labor or birth. That is why it is so tragic about twins. I think the men made the taboo around twins—because a double gift would be too much for the women to give each other. But no explanation has ever been made to me about this. It is what I think." Margery spoke slowly, sometimes lying back upon her flung-out arm. Lily listened breathlessly, moving closer to listen because the words came out rhythmically and paced, but slowly with effort. Margery turned suddenly, their faces close. "Do you think they make each other beautiful for the men? Oh, there is a dimension of sorcery to it, no doubt. The men know that and fear it, they arrange marriages, create jealousies by showering favors on one and depriving another." In the darkness, Margery sat up, slipping out of the rest of her thin dress; turned back to lie against Lily who gasped as skin touched skin. Carefully she felt for Margery's breasts.

Margery did not move away from Lily's caress, even as she continued speaking. " Women hold a great deal of power in their bonding. Mkumi recognized this long before I came here. Some say she poisoned her husband to make her power greater. Some say she is barren because of that. Some say she has great power because she defied the stigma of barreness, and her husband died because that power surpassed him. I think not—she looked around her and kept bonds where they might have otherwise been broken. That is why she can sit with Shiwezi. She is an enlightened woman and will be remembered for a long time by her people even if she conjures up a healthy fear now. You know what she said to me the first day you arrived?"

"What?"

"She said simply, pointing, 'There she is.' I didn't know what she meant until I went up on the mountain with you. She cackled when she said it. There she is."

"Then it is she...." Lily whispered as she put her arms gently around Margery, her fingers playing there on her back, feeling the muscles beneath skin, "she is the one who conjured me."

"So that I think you are flesh and blood? This is quite possible—I would think she is quite capable of such a thing." Margery smiled in the dark, looking down at her. "I wish I had a pillow for you, Lily. I would spread your long tresses like a halo all about on it."

All the while it rained they lay together so, caressing each other until stripped bare of their clothing, their fear, their past, their country, their queen.

And in the morning it was still raining, their bodies still entwined, sleepless, but dreaming.

"I'm getting rained on," Lily grumbled. "It's dripping on my head."

"Then come closer to me," said Margery sleepily, pulling Lily to one side of the bed.

"The bed is getting wet."

"Of course, darling. It always does when it rains, warm and wet, hm, so it isn't something to fret about. And if it is raining we can linger because that is the custom. There will be no palaver today, and Chief Zwem is surely cursing that he does not have Shiwezi to lie with. You understand now how fortunate this storm has been, all the way around." Then she added, "Though I am sure he will have found some-one else for the time being. After all, he can't begrudge a woman her time apart if she is bleeding. He cannot touch her then on any account. Chief Zwem expects nothing for a week, but then he will begin to chafe."

"A week. Won't we talk to him before that?"

"Well, not today at any rate. I only want to concern myself with you."

## 17.

A commotion outside had Margery up and dressed even before 'Mgamelele came to the hut hurriedly. Lily dressed as well.

"Oh dear," said Margery said as she poked her head out the door, "it's Nakala, Chief Zwem's personal witch-doctor come to rattle his feathers. He could hardly wait for the rain to stop, eh? Brace yourself."

Before Lily had time to inquire why, Margery had disappeared. And as usual, all she could do was follow, observe.

The witch-doctor had already aroused the others of the village into what Lily knew was a seething panic, what with their drawn faces, their rigid bodies, their wide eyes. The children curious but in retreat, peered from the relative safety of the hut doorways. And all the while the thatch still dripping.

He stalked around the perimeter of the courtyard to which he was clearly not invited while Margery went to stand purposefully in the center of it, hands on her hips, looking upon him as disdainfully as he gazed upon her. His motions were slow and stylistic in a prescribed dance of intimidation. In full regalia of feathers, dangling skins of various kinds of cats, amulets and pouches of secrets, he reeked of stale sweat, smoke and a sickeningly sweet musk. No doubt he had smeared the excretion of some kind of animal gland, often from male antelopes, all over himself.

With some relief, Lily noticed that Mbo had come to stand beside her, protectively even as he twitched.

A shouting match between Margery and the witch-doctor ensued in Faung as they exchanged well-matched insults.

"What are they saying?" Lily hissed to Mbo who flinched.

"Bad word, bad word."

"Why?"

"She say he is meat for the crocs. He say he not hear woman with no child."

"Mm. A barren woman."

Mbo pointed. "She laugh, Ma. She say she has many children. He say they have the curse. She say, yes, danger, danger for him."

Lily listened intently, catching some of the words, frustrated but appreciative of Mbo's translation which was as broken in English as she ever managed in Faung. How she longed for at least a fluency of comprehension with this drama before her.

'Mgamelele moved from where she stood near the courtyard wall like a chess piece, into the center slightly behind Margery. The witch-doctor squatted, spat in the dirt, began to trace a circle and pull out objects from one of his many leather pouches.

Margery turned to Lily, "Our Chief Zwem has obviously found out that something is up. Nakala's unpleasant presence is going to be keeping things unsettled here for awhile, especially since Mkumi is absent. I wonder, how would you feel about taking over for her with Shiwezi? 'Mgamelele can go with you. Do you think you can manage?"

"Absolutely. But what harm can he do?"

"You'd be surprised, make my whole village sick. Don't underestimate his power of suggestion. At this point he is here mostly for show, but it is no charade, believe me."

"I'm off then." Lily ducked back into the hut for her hat. I am a trader, she thought, isn't this why I have these packs of beads, liquor, what-not? Let me trade then, one way or another. And taking a small knife from her portmanteau, she also carefully removed some lace from her undergarments. Packing items in a basket, she picked out a bottle of rum, letting the weight of it rest in her hand as she appraised it. She did not know Margery's opinion about liquor, nor did she wish to find out, not if it meant the same kind of exchange as they had had over the revolver. Placing the items in a small bag which she slung onto her shoulder, she checked her revolver before tucking it well into her sash.

When she re-emerged she saw Margery settling herself into a squat, staring at her opponent. As Lily brushed passed her, Margery put out a hand, gripping Lily's arm firmly, then releasing it.

"You are not afraid, are you, Lily?"

Lily shook her head resolutely. "Not afraid, no, I wouldn't describe myself as such. Angry, yes."

"Good," said Margery with a dismissive nod of her head, a fleeting flash of affection in her glance, "use it in good stead but don't do anything rash. Please, keep your head about you."

"I will."

"Are you sure you haven't forgotten your pith helmet and Bible?"

Stopping mid-stride, Lily rallied. "My parasol and revolver, you mean."

"Ah, it's just that you look like a woman with a mission."

"That I am."

"Then go to it."

With that Lily—her liquor and lace—and 'Mgamelele began walking swiftly down the path to the river. Mbo and Peta hastened after her, but she turned them away.

"I am going to the women's compound where you cannot come. Please stay here, or take the others and go off on a hunt, if you wish."

Mbo's downcast face brightened quickly.

"If you can find something suitable for me to present to Chief Zwem, it would be a good thing. Take as many days as you need."

"Yes Ma."

She smiled her farewell because she knew he was happy, and most eager to get out of the village for awhile.

Utter nonsense, utter nonsense to proceed, eh Fitzipatriki? she thought as she strode impatiently. Here I am in the thick of it, and I didn't even manage to have any tea. Will rum suffice?

The two women clambered aboard a dug-out, 'Mgamelele

141

steering while Lily paddled in the bow, observing that crocodiles made a counter movement as if they had a plan worked out—one canoe wasn't much to bother about, so only two slipped into the water while the rest of the hoard stayed on the sandbanks sunning themselves. Probably the two hungriest, Lily surmised, bashing one of them on the snout as it came bobbing up. Forgetting the Faung idiom, she barked angrily, "Bugger off."

In the back of the canoe she heard 'Mgamelele chuckling, more like a throaty cackle. Turning, she grinned back, not knowing she had proffered so catchy a phrase until 'Mgamelele repeated it, a thickly Faung version, 'Bugga offi,' for the rest for the journey, until they were both shouting it in raucous unison, laughing, their paddles smacking the water each time.

Lily wondered what it would be like to relate the incident someday to Audrey. The expression came from her after all, as she battered the poor butcher boy out of the kitchen time and again.

By the time they reached the opposite bank, Lily felt that her alliance with 'Mgamelele was further cemented, even though their ability to converse remained limited.

They came upon Chief Zwem camped out at the entrance pathway to the women's compound like a cat waiting at a mouse-hole.

My my, thought Lily, this has become an obsession, totally out of hand. Surrounded by his usual entourage of elders and age-mates, he sat on his three-legged throne. All of them seemed to be undertaking their usual pastimes together, it was simply that he had moved court to a strategic place.

She passed through their gathering, their steady gazes boring into her; she didn't think it was an opportune occasion to trade. But there had to be some way to present Chief Zwem with a portion of rum in such a way that he would not be suspicious, that he would take it as a gesture of good will. But how could there be any good will if Shiwezi didn't want to marry him?

And what was Shiwezi thinking today about it all? How could she possibly make up her mind with all this brewing around her? All the while without her child.

Making her way with 'Mgamelele through the under-growth, ducking passed menacing fetishes, under low gates of brambles and woven grass, calling out obligatory greetings, she finally entered the clearing into the women's compound once again. Way back on the Oguye she had thought of such a place as cause for celebration. Here she entered, sensing the possible hostility. Once she had been embraced within a tribe, here she was the intruder, breaking rules, stirring up trouble.

The scene was peaceful enough. Mkumi had brought fresh bamboo grass for Shiwezi who was weaving mats. How deftly her dark fingers moved as she sat there self-contained just as she had when Lily first met up with her. If she languished, it was within a persistent industry. We are like that, sighed Lily, we are like that everywhere. The pain is buried in silence while we toil away, our handiwork screaming out that we exist, whether its boiling laundry, scrubbing floors, pounding grain or weaving a mat.

She greeted both Mkumi and Shiwezi but let 'Mgamelele do the explaining, while feeling at a loss that she couldn't rely on a solid interpreter to convey her own thoughts.

"I stay here with you," was about all she could manage.

At the mere mention of Nakala, Mkumi's face took on the scowl of a brewing storm. Rising stiffly, she seemed to gather herself together much like Queen Victoria might swoosh off in her gown, Lily acknowledged, but rather than a rustle of silk, there was the rattle of bones, the jingle of bracelets.

Lily wanted to rush along with her and see what would happen, but she too was confined now like Shiwezi. She looked more closely around her at the compound. Three dilapidated huts stood recently, but untidily thatched, and in bad need of redaubing. The walls which were cracked and falling into dust, revealed their skeletal structures of wattle. She could hear low voices from the farthest hut but no one emerged, even as they kept watch over her and Shiwezi. What was the matter with the women of Chief Zwem's village that their compound was so shabby and forlorn? Melancholy hung about in the patches of smoke from their fires caught in the hollows between the huts.

Pacing around the edge of the compound like a prisoner's first inspection of a cell, Lily pondered the thick vegetation. A few paths seemed to slip away here and there into the forest, but she had no way of knowing how far they went. Her experience with these kind of paths was that they led to an ancestral fetish, gloomy and laden with fast decaying offerings, or else were used to find a place to relieve oneself. She had taken such paths many times to try and find a private place.

If only she could guarantee that one led all the way to the river. Usually the women's compound only had one entrance, no rabbit-hole exits. How could fetishes be expected to guard two such forbidden paths? And yet she circled, beating away the flies, pondering each path's direction without really stopping. Shiwezi went on with her mats, but glanced up occasionally.

Squinting at the sun, Lily tried to determined the direction of the river. What if they managed to slip away, at night perhaps, when no one in their right mind ventured anywhere? What if she took Shiwezi out of there and all the way back to Margery's village?

She needed a scythe; she needed a canoe down by the river. Would the moon-light be enough? Could they follow the river bank until they found a dug-out?

The more she paced around, the more impatient and compelled she felt. She had had enough confinement in her life. The memory of all the days and nights she had stayed in her family home gripped her very core. She had come to Africa to be free of all that, to get far away into the open wilderness where nothing could contain her! She did not belong to this society with its complex web of rules and restraints, anymore than she wanted to belong to her own culture. They seemed equally arbitrary to her, both bent on keeping people in bondage.

Surely she hadn't defied all those restrictions back home just to find herself where she was—pacing the perimeter of the compound. No, she had discovered that boundaries could dissipate. And with Margery, she had released the inner shackles of her soul.

144

And hadn't Shiwezi defied boundaries too? Shiwezi had travelled alone with a child. What had compelled her to go on then—attempting to surpass a communal if not universal curse? Could she not be compelled to act again?

Lily stopped and eyed the young woman sitting there in seeming passivity, only her hands dancing with the grasses.

How do I communicate this? Lily asked when about all I know is to say 'Come along with me.'

She made an inspection of the compound again, spying a few scythes of beaten metal which must have been used in the recent thatching. They were stacked against the wall of a hut, behind a large mortar and pestle.

Which would be a better time, dusk or dawn? If Mkumi was in the throes of battle with Nakala and Chief Zwem, how long would it take for them to find out that Shiwezi had left the women's compound? How long would it take to reach Margery's? It was simple; they had to make their escape by night. Most large snakes were coiled up at that time, but big cats were about. She shuddered at the memory of the leopard, the spring waiting in its haunches, the cold calculation in its tawny eyes.

I must call upon its stealth, she thought, closing her eyes, her fingers clasping her own personal pouch that 'Llile had made long ago for her, and the piece of leopard ear Peta had given her to put in it. What I don't sense, Shiwezi will know.

Then the drums began, a long, slow, repetitive and dreary rhythm. Lily couldn't resist the tug of them, and made her way, tripping hurriedly back down the path. But she did not show herself, instead remained just out of view of Chief Zwem's impromptu court, watching through the foliage that screened her. There, the chief sat as before with his elders, except that now, more of the villagers had arrived, along with drummers, and set up a circle. Blimey, she cursed. Nakala was there, dancing dirge-like on the bare earth of the arena in front of his chief. It certainly hadn't taken him long to make his way back over the river. Another stand-off! This time with Mkumi hurling the insults back at him, her speech rapid and musical, like an anti-dote to the drums which beat and beat on. It was almost as bad as all those wailing women back at the French mission—with one exception. This was male magic. Very definitely, she decided—the drumming ground into her soul. She could feel it, and mustered her concentration back to Mkumi's voice rising against that low, heavy rhythm. The diviner's voice was like water tumbling off rocks, but dangerous rocks—like those the river rapids beat against in froth. The kind that split boats up the middle.

Villagers were still swarming into position on the periphery, bringing along firewood. It was going to last a good while. Turning she lumbered back up the path into the womens' compound; but there was no getting away. She was imprisoned by the beating.

By this time the heat was getting the better of Lily, so she went to sit down on a large root under a wild nut tree near Shiwezi who remained in the full sun. Taking the canvas pack from her shoulder, she opened it a drew out the bottle of rum. If only she could present the rum to Chief Zwem and have him see it as a gesture of good-will, not something to treat with suspicion. If only she could jot of a note of 'kind regards.'

And all the while those infernal drums. Her decision was simple and final: We have to get out of this place. We will break the bonds of even the sound.

She went over to sit by Shiwezi, quietly broaching the idea of her plan in her paltry Faung. "Shi Robolo—the river, where is it?"

Shiwezi tilted her head, flicked her hand to the northwest.

Good, thought Lily, just as I thought; she brooded on the words she knew because she didn't want to use any signs that the women in the hut could interpret. "Shiwezi and Lily, we go to the river, find canoe. We go to Woman with Lights. We go when the sun sets."

Shiwezi's face remained unmoving, but Lily could see the young woman's intelligence flashing in those liquid eyes as she tried to make sense of Lily's preposterous plan. And she could see the fear as well.

"Crocodiles," Shiwezi returned simply, nodding her head sharply.

"Of course, I hadn't thought of that." Lily said in English.

"How the hell can we find our way along the river. If it isn't one bloody thing it's another...."

There was a pause in the high pitched refrain that Mkumi had sustained. A pause in the drumming. Quick shouts and ululations—the latter came from 'Mgamelele, didn't they? Lily's heart skipped. She realized she was bracing herself—for what? And then the drumming began again, smooth, relentless. And with them, Mkumi's voice, strong, unwavering.

Lily felt Shiwezi's hand on her arm, looked into her eyes and saw a fierce resolve there. My god, she's going to take it on! Lily wanted to jump up in jubilation but held herself tightly. We will do it, by Fitzi- patriki, we're going to do it. God, she must be desperate. Who'd want to stay in this dreary place; it isn't a happy place for women.

Shiwezi let go, rose to her feet and walked towards the stack of scythes. Lily watched, puzzled, alarmed that Shiwezi would make a move for one of them now. Shortly, she returned to Lily, handing her the one she had picked out. She pointed to her dwindling supply of bamboo grass, then like a prisoner trying to tell a jailer how to be free to go in and out, pointed to the compound path where Lily could go in search of grass to cut.

Pleased with herself that she understood, Lily took the scythe in delight. Of course, it was a simple tool, not a forbidden weapon. She paused, wanting to explore some of the side paths. She turned, pointing to one of them which in all likelihood would bring them close to the the river, but Shiwezi quickly turned her back towards the main path.

Of course, nitwit, Lily scolded herself. To go anywhere else would leave Shiwezi vulnerable. Zwem's watchful wives and relatives would drag her right off to him. So Lily made her way down the path, investigating as she went. After scooting through some of the low gates, she came to a thicket of bamboo grass which tended to grow up in old clearings, the stalks taller than she was, and began to cut. Oddly enough, she didn't want to be far from Shiwezi now, as though something might come between them. As she whacked the grass, pulling out the loose bunches, a shadowy figure jumped out at her, its eyes protruding, barring

147

her way. Bloody hell—the drums were waking the dead!

She reeled at its suddenness, as though she had lifted an invisible curtain. A shudder went through her as though the leopard had sprung upon Masa all over again. There in the overgrown grass loomed a fetish which seemed to shrink just as suddenly before her eyes into a small carving on a pedestal of stone. She gasped, frightened. My mind is playing tricks on me, she scolded herself, but for a moment the figure had been alive—she knew it. And off course, that's why there was grass here, springing up around what had been cleared away. The place was literally populated with hidden statues, all to ward off intruders who might try circuitous detours. They sprung up like demons.

This particular statue of a woman had only the stains of offerings left on it, the poisons permeating the wood enough to ward off termites. Had it been someone's personal statue, someone dead a long time ago, and therefor left in peace—or left due to fear?

Whatever, Lily found it a most opportune discovery, in part because the statue itself was not much larger than a rum bottle. The enlarged head held bold protruding eyes which often represented uncanny sight or vision. She felt compelled to believe that she had found her guide for the forest escape, an ally in her scheme. The head-dress showed a coil of beaded hair depicting a woman of rank. The body of the statue was disproportionately small, arms suggested alongside the torso, but with prominent breasts, protruding belly and an undeniably etched vulva. Carefully dislodging it from its pedestal, she placed it in her bag. Yes, she would claim it as her own protector, this spirit found in the grasses, and which either the drums or Mkumi's song had surely alerted.

With a large bundle of hay that she hoped wasn't too tick infested, Lily trundled back to Shiwezi, feverish with the presence of her statue in the bag, and the prospect of escape. Heart thudding, she let down in relief when she saw Shiwezi sitting there as before, weaving.

# 18.

As dusk fell, Shiwezi who had brought back wood, built up a fire, while Lily went to sit in the doorway of the hut that had become Shiwezi's over the days, and which no one else wanted to share. They bided their time until the other women and children seemed to have settled in their hut. From the thick aroma that hung on the smoke from that direction, beer was brewing.

"Picnic time," mumbled Lily, removing her canvas pouch which she set carefully at the edge of the fire pit, pulling out her statue and tucking it in her sash. The bottle of rum, she made stick out of the bag, draping the strands of lace about it like a calling card. Rolling up her two completed mats and slinging them on her back, Shiwezi led the way; quietly as darkness set in, each of them wielding a scythe, the two escapees slipped into the deep shadows of the forest, leaving the drums to beat far behind them.

With her bare feet, Shiwezi sensed the path, vegetation continually arching across their passage at waist and shoulder height. Lily was glad not to have a light; it was much better not knowing what snakes hung about from branches above their heads, or what eyes might be peering at them through the leaves. Brandishing her statue in her left hand, her fingers tight and clammy, it was as though the 'uncanny vision' would see what danger she had to avoid.

While the drumming surged and faded in their wake, the path petered out, but she expected that. Now they had to rely on Shiwezi's judgment as the younger woman forged ahead, slicing branches and the constant curtain of vines out of the way. Ever so often she would stand stock still to listen to the forest noises around them. Tree frogs were constant, but they made out the distant cough cough of a leopard, enough to send shivers down Lily's spine, but not enough to deter her. Then they would proceed, stop again.

The ground changed underfoot, becoming spongier. Marsh grasses, high as their heads, took over from the trees so that they could even glimpse the stars emerging above as the darkness set in, no moon for the present.

Tense, the surface of her body tingling, she followed Shiwezi, alert, even euphoric the further they went. She kept on thinking they would find pursuers hot on their heels, but behind them the forest closed upon itself, as foreboding as the way ahead. Her only hope and consolation was that all the villagers were surely distracted for the time-being. In that sense, the ever-permeating drums were re-assuring, though she couldn't catch Mkumi's voice any longer.

Surely it wasn't that far to the river if they were already encountering wet bogs. What remained critical was not to find any bodies of back-water, but to keep on firm ground for as long as possible. Did Shiwezi know where she was going? She seemed to double-back as she searched for footing.

As Lily's feet began to sink more, further up her calf, she hitched her skirt up around her waist, tying it in a knot to one side.

Shiwezi stopped suddenly, bracing Lily with her arm. A moment later they heard the mild plop of a crocodile entering water to their left, perhaps twenty feet away, Lily couldn't tell for certain; she hoped it was further away than that. It was enough of a warning that Shiwezi began to pick her way carefully.

They got used to the sounds of crocodiles lashing in the water, but as they moved, Lily despaired that they were proceeding too far inland again, and would end up smack in the middle of the village. And yet she could not hear any voices, nor smell smoke, taking small comfort in that fact.

Slowly, slowly they seemed to be bending back to the left again and on towards the river proper. Once again they entered forest and drier ground. She tired to remember the walk up from the canoe launch; how many paces to the village? Surely, they should be coming upon canoes soon; how long it was taking.

Once again they began skirting a backwash, pushing their way through the grasses, the sharp leaves lacerating their faces and forearms. Lily much preferred the feel of cobwebs after Shiwezi had brushed away the spiders. And as the heavy dew set in much like a drizzle, she braced herself against the chill. But there was no chill; the air was warm and heavy. The chill came from within herself, her jaws dancing, even though her heart seemed to pummel her body.

At last she could see the black glint of water through the trees. They stalked gingerly towards the bank to scout around for crocodiles, but more so, to see if they could spot any canoes, even the tell-tale sound of water lapping, or one canoe thudding against another. Back again to the thick cover of trees, ferns and knotted vines.

Her eyesight was finally adjusting to the deep night; she knew now that the many black logs that littered the banks were much more lethal than anything that flood waters would deposit anywhere. She was glad that crocodiles did not wander in search of grass the way hippos did, and that the hippos were said to be down-river.

She might have worried about many mammalian dangers, but what really took the toll was the constant cloud of mosquitoes, thicker and more unbearable than any of the vegetation they tore through, unbearable because there was no relief. After awhile Lily wondered if she could hear any other sound but the buzzing in her ears.

A guttural squeak from Shiwezi made Lily's head reel. Somehow they had met up with a path, well worn enough to be more than a game trail. Excitedly, Shiwezi made a left turn, tugging on Lily's arm, as they hastened once again towards the river.

There, unmistakable, were at least half a dozen dug-outs lashed to the stakes of a fishing weir, but bobbing in the water, butting each other with the undulations of the river. It seemed possible to make their way and claim one without running into crocodiles which usually had to be yelled at, sometimes prodded to crawl away, using the usual long paddles. The only question was whether any paddles were in the canoes, as often the villagers took theirs home with them, some being highly personal items.

A quick inspection revealed no paddles, so Lily kept a fretful watch while Shiwezi back-tracked into the forest in the search for specific saplings of the right height. One by one she dragged a few trees back to the bank, then set about with her scythe to strip off the small branches. Paddle blades were often fashioned from a separate piece of wood, then fitted into the pole which had been sliced up the middle. Once the blade was in place it was secured with twine.

More rudimentary paddles could be fashioned by pounding the root end of the tree until it was somewhat flattened. This is what Shiwezi proceeded to do, every blow setting Lily on edge, for fear the sound would travel, echoing across the river, and cause alarm. Then she realized that Shiwezi was working to the cover of each distant drum-beat, resting, listening, resuming. Dull and intermittent, Shiwezi pounded with the handle of her scythe, the chore taking an excruciatingly long time. Too long. Keeping a canoe ready to push out was foremost on Lily's mind; Shiwezi could not hand her the first paddle soon enough. They would do with one if they had to. But at last, with what was surely a deafening whack— enough to rouse an entire village from its preoccupation, Shiwezi seemed to think the second one was fit enough. She motioned for Lily to get in, and once settled, took to pushing the canoe out, gracefully taking the stern.

Out on the river they had some scope, still no moon. And as if surprised out of sleep, the tell-tale ridges of a few crocodiles broke the surface of the inky water to follow them. The women battled the current up-river, but were unable to make out the main launch of canoes against the black river bank. Slowly they battled their way across the river to the other side, trying to find familiar landmarks in the ghostly terrain, Lily's wooden guardian facing the prow. Only in midstream did they come somewhat clear of the mosquitoes, Lily's body now on fire with the myriad of bites she had incurred, made more acute as the sweat built up on her skin in her labor. Her head beginning to pound.

All she wanted to do was to get back to Margery, find eventual respite under the canopy of mosquito netting. It was a simple dream.

In spite of the clouds of mosquitoes they had to hug the bank to find their way. Finally with a subdued yelp she announced the sighting of their familiar canoe launch, right near the great deposit of clay that the women of the village dug into almost daily. Poling the canoe up to the bank, Lily clambered out, pulling in the prow so Shiwezi could follow. Then with a quick decision, she released the canoe and paddles for the river to take away—better not hold onto a canoe that would later incur debt.

Her head splitting by now but silently elated, Lily hooked arms with Shiwezi as they made their way up the wide path. Then Lily stopped, wasn't there a path cut somewhere about, a different trail cut specifically for the tainted woman with the baby on that first day she had met up with Margery? Could she find it in the dark? If so, they would take it and be assured of the protection of defilement, of curse. Who would appear there to accost them or bar the way? Slowing her pace, she glanced about for the suggestive opening of a rude path, so recently hacked out. She had seen its beginning next to a gnarled and ancient tree of a species she didn't know.

Finally, she recognized the tree, felt along the bark as she peered to find the path. And did it not stand open for them? As she turned aside to take it, Shiwezi balked, standing still as a fetish.

"Come," Lily pleaded in Faung. "No curses, no curses for us here." She could only hope that the words she picked had the right nuance for the situation. There were many words for curses, a different set for anything defiled.

Shiwezi seemed to consider the message, proceeding behind in that subdued pace Lily had encountered before, slow and resistant, not at all the brazen scythe-wielder on the opposite bank.

"No people, no enemies," Lily ventured lamely. "We rest here, wait till the sun comes." She pointed to what looked like a spot of grasses. Taking her scythe, she sliced at the stalks, trying to make a matting for them to lie down on. She wanted badly to rest, depleted from the anxiety she had carried as her burden, feeling sick from her headache, and the incessant drumming—she couldn't tell if she truly heard them or simply had the echo in her brain. Whichever, it was important to be composed when they made their eventual entrance into Margery's village. Only now when they had made it safely across the river, did she balk at what reaction she might receive.

Shiwezi sat down heavily, panting, wiping her face with her arms.

Tucked away, they both sat hanging their heads, Lily rocking back and forth to keep her mind off the hot hives all over her body; tried to comfort herself by singing softly, "We did it, we did it." Cradling the fetish in her hands, she kissed its wooden forehead, before tucking it away in her sash.

Perhaps she dozed off, because it wasn't the cacophony of monkeys and birds which woke her but the sound of human voices that jolted her awake in the pre-dawn. Shiwezi who had fallen asleep in a fetal position with her mats for a pillow, sat bolt upright as well. Their eyes met, mirroring each other's dazed alarm. But the voices, close at hand, called out in motion to running feet; it had to be either hunters or fishermen heading out into the damp morning, nothing more. The sounds came close but passed on swiftly on separate unseen paths. Lily had been right to seek refuge on the defiled path. Something else was noticeable—the sound of distant, throbbing drums had ceased; how still the forest seemed by contrast with its innocent hum of creatures about their business.

She shook Shiwezi's shoulder reassuringly, before pulling herself up. It was time to present themselves in the village where they belonged, Lily believing now that Shiwezi was mistress of herself.

Together they walked up the path.

"Heavens," Margery said, looking up from her morning tea—and she could not hide her genuine surprise. "What have we here? You must be an angel. No, you must be a sorceress, an angelic sorceress? I thought I told you to keep your head about you. What have you done?"

"Returned," said Lily simply as if her dishevelment, what with her hair half-undone, was a matter of course, and only now realizing that she had lost one of her combs "I want a pot of tea." She spoke while intently watching Shiwezi who walked into the courtyard, straight to Mtoli. He was sitting on a mat, eating squash with his hands; looked up at her with outstretched arms. Laughing, the mother swung him up to her breast, crooning at him. Lily could see his small fingers come around her back, kneading her skin.

"You want a pot of tea," Margery repeated, "when what you're handing me is a fine kettle of fish. I don't suppose you'd mind telling me what happened?"

"Certainly not. It was simple, really. Neither of us wanted to stay there anymore, so we came home. And don't think I dragged her back, if she hadn't hacked the way through, we wouldn't be here."

"Hm, and you look to be in a sorry state for it. I will get you poultices for your skin. What is that in your hand—some curio to take back to London?"

"My spiritual guide," Lily held up the statue and smiled. "We met near the compound after she jumped out at me— she was quite neglected, you know, grass all around her. I took her, with all due respect, to guide my way in the dark, as I did not have one of your lights."

"How presumptuous of you," Margery joked lightly, then said seriously, "She may well not have been neglected but hidden away due to her powers. Mkumi will know who she is. Watch out you don't cause fear and trembling with that statue." She took it into her hands, running her fingers over the contour, crooning as if to a baby, "Yes, you haven't been touched in a long time, have you—to be neglected so. She is quite fearsome, is she not, Lily? Look how both the lips of her mouth and her sex are so similar, at right angles to each, swollen with power. Mkumi maintains that no woman is barren if she can swell with such fertile power."

Lily's reeled with Margery's direct talk, shaken but fascinated as she stood staring down at the statue, more so, at the movements of Margery's hands upon it.

"I hope you are strong enough to sustain her power along side you. How the hell did you get here anyway?"

"That's the first I have heard you swear," Lily chided, startled. "We came the hard way believe me, forging through the undergrowth like two wild beasts until we found a place on the river that had canoes."

"You weren't transported on some miraculous cloud ?"

"No, only through the dark."

"Well, it shall be taken for black magic no matter what you say."

"Speaking of black magic—what's with Nakala?"

"Oh, he left yesterday after you. They were obviously in a stand-off all night. Now the drumming has stopped—nasty stuff, that drumming. They'll be back. Indeed, they'll be back in full force now. I don't suppose you took that into consideration?"

Lily fetched herself some tea in the cracked cup and sank down onto the low wall gratefully. "I'll face events as they come. I simply couldn't stay there any longer, Margery."

Only now did Margery gently put her hand over Lily's. "Impatience is a European virtue, eh? And you, all scraped up. Your hair is a mess. I will comb it." And Margery did with Lily's remaining comb. "It has been a long time since I combed hair like this. When my cousin came to visit we used to brush and brush each other's hair. We'd read seemier parts of the Bible—spilling seed...David watching Bathsheba bathe and all that— always finding them by mistake, but never forgetting where they were. We learned a lot that we would not have known any other way."

"Your lessons in human nature," Lily laughed and tilted her head back. "Did it prepare you for all this?"

"Not at all." Margery tugged playfully on a lock of hair

"Ow," Lily protested, pulling her head away to no avail. "Has Mbo returned yet?"

"No, but Ngobi stayed behind. You must see him. They told me he has the fever, but I think it is something else. Perhaps he is feeling homesick. He wears such a sour expression, just sits outside the hut or lies about inside."

Lily turned in the direction of the men's hut as Margery played with the strand of her hair and combed it out. "He doesn't look sick to me. He's standing anyway."

"Really?" Margery glanced about. "Gracious, would you look at that? He must be glad you are back."

Lily followed the direction of his gaze, and found it to be upon Shiwezi. "No, I don't think so. I think he has been love-sick. Except that notion would challenge your theory that they aren't romantic."

"Theory!" Margery retorted, as she pulled loose a snarl. "I have no theories. Just remember that. I just watch. I told you before—how do we recognize what we don't know, unless we see it, or see anew?"

"Perhaps some things are universal, as is our love."

"Mmm—my romantic," Margery kissed the nape of Lily's neck as she scooped up her hair, securing it in a loose bun with the comb. "Well, now you have another problem. If Ngobi is indeed smitten by Shiwezi, are you going to give her into marriage to him?"

Lily stood up. "How do I know? It depends on Shiwezi, doesn't it?"

"Better find out. It could put a new twist on an already complicated situation."

## 19.

With cool, leafy poultices on her burning, itchy skin, Lily slowly revived herself in the shade of the courtyard, while Margery tended to the children, and returned later with a contrite looking Ngobi trailing behind her.

"He wants to marry her," Margery announced, "but he has no dowry, so of course he sees his emotions as useless, as good as death. Never would he have ever volunteered such a wish—I had to drag it out of him by saying you were most unhappy with the raid and all. He wants to know if, when he receives his wages from you, whether that will be enough, because that is what he has to offer—plus wishing to remind you, with the deepest respect, that he has been a very good porter, and helpful in all duties, that during his employment with you, he has not become unmanageably drunk."

"Please tell him I understand," Lily rallied and sat up. "That yes indeed, he has been a strong member of the expedition, but that I cannot offer him anything until we have talked with Shiwezi. And yet how do I know if he will truly answer for her? How do I know he won't beat her if I am not present to watch for her well-being?"

Margery nodded, then prattled away at length, and Ngobi responded soberly. "He says he will be a good husband, and wants many children who will know and sing your name, and that you need have no fear for Shiwezi, nor for Mtoli—he will raise him as his own. "

Shiwezi was summoned then, and Ngobi's proposal put forth to her. She stood shyly, her shoulders sagging, her head bowed, her baby tucked and sleeping on her back. With a nervous giggle, she heard Margery out, punctuating the flow of words with responsive hums, and clicks. At last she answered, and Lily thought she understood enough to know it was affirmative.

Margery smiled. "There. She says she likes this much better than Chief Zwem, if she and Ngobi can stay here. Say, it might be pleasant to have a man about the house, mmm.... You were right—they have been noticing each other for sometime, probably flirting right under your nose!"

"Undoubtedly, and not even subtly I suppose. What would I know?"

"Hm. They have already slept together, so their request now is not unfounded, as they find each other compatible."

"When the hell did they do that?" sputtered Lily, trying to cover her sense of shock, her naivete, and resulting indignation. It was a sensibility that clung to her from her past, because had she not herself recently lain with Margery and found it honest, acceptable? And did she not want to again? Then why couldn't Shiwezi be so smitten too? Still, what stunned Lily was the realization that Shiwezi may have been driven by other passions during the night than for Mtoli.

"Surprised, are we? I don't see why. It was during the festivities when Shiwezi made the beer. Ngobi says you are a great woman because you have brought Shiwezi back. Indeed, my dear, I think he might have curled up and died, literally, if Chief Zwem had had his way. And Nakala would have felt he had done something consequential."

"But why then did he not answer for her?"

"You know the why—what claim did he have? With a betrothal, all this changes. She becomes immune."

"Then that is what we shall do."

"Ah, but Chief Zwem has a prior claim. Don't forget that— we have to settle with him first."

Lily's jubilation melted into weariness. The two women excused themselves, and returned to the courtyard shade, followed by some of the children while Lily watched Ngobi and Shiwezi go off in separate directions without even a sideways glance.

To herself Lily thought, I will simply say that Shiwezi is not for trade and that she is to marry a man in my party. If they have slept together already, it is they who have a prior claim. She could bloody-well be carrying a child already.

Not since her mother's sick bed had she felt trapped, bound so to a place the way she found herself now, bound by her thoughts, and bound by events beyond her control. Under any other circumstances, she would have simply proceeded on with her party, having not set up a situation ripe for a raid in the first place. But here she was, captivated by Margery, wanting only to be with her, and at the same time finding herself immediately caught up in a web of life, somehow beyond her scope as a temporary vagabond. And if and when there was resolution, wouldn't it be time to go?

The song of successful hunters coming up the path brought her round to the moment. Everyone in the village turned alert faces towards the singing, and sang back in response, the children running down the path eagerly to join the procession. Lily listen carefully, knowing these songs by now, and picked out the two refrains: "'We have brought meat, like the leopard we brought a buck down, with our skill and prowess we brought him down,' and 'We have found honey in the forest, honey dripping from the trees; we have found honey, in our cleverness we have outwitted the bees.'"

Margery applauded the mention of honey. "It has been a long time. Something like this doesn't just happen, you know, it can only be taken as a good sign. You have brought Christmas with you again and again, darling." Smiling, she bent down and kissed Lily on the forehead, then bustled about the courtyard, unfurling mats for everyone to sit on.

Honey made for a joyous diversion as Mbo presented the great bulb of comb, upset bees still clinging to it. He flicked them off into the fire pit with the tip of his spear, and using leaves that the children had swiftly plucked—as though they had swooped china plates from a cupboard—he began to dole out chunks for them.

"I can't eat the honey that way," Margery sighed, "it's the larvae in the comb—I just can't quite—but a spoonful in my tea, I live for that."

Lily laughed. "You live for your tea as it is, this is simply going to spoil you!"

With all the distraction, Lily almost forgot her recent trek. Relaxing in the shade, she closed her eyes, re-applying the cool poultice to her face while listening to the hubbub around her, Mbo's voice recounting the hunt, and the children's squeals of joy in response. And so it was that Mkumi arrived, surprised at the sight of Lily, Margery going out to embrace her in greeting. Only then was Lily's attention drawn to their rapid conversation. Mkumi did not look as though she were angry or bothered as Lily expected somehow; instead she was laughing.

Margery waved agitatedly to Lily, bringing Mkumi along, arms entwined as she called out, "What is this I hear? Chief Zwem is very happy with the satchel you left behind, more so for the spirit-water you left him in an invisible calabash. What business do you think you have bringing liquor into the interior?"

Lily was put on guard for an instant but she was slowly growing used to this with Margery. She replied, "I am here to trade, you know."

"It has gotten you out of the fix over Shiwezi—I'll say that much for you. He is quite well aware that she isn't in his domain anymore so his position in the negotiation has been greatly reduced. His wives ran out to him first thing this morning to announce that you had vanished. Much to do! But you have another fix—since his brother was in debt to him, paid off by the raid on Shiwezi, now his brother has come into debt once again. You are in debt to his brother because of your actions. Fortunately, Chief Zwem will be very happy if you can provide him with more of this liquor of yours. I hope you have a fair stock of it because a little is not going to satisfy such a big debt."

Lily beamed. "I think that Chief Zwem and I can begin to trade. There is nothing I would like better." But she wondered just how big a debt she had incurred. Somehow she felt as though it might be limitless.

Margery hugged Mkumi, looking at her fondly. "You also have Mkumi to thank for explaining that the liquor was not poison, and even trying some herself to prove its benevolent power. Thank God, they don't know how drunk it can make

161

them—yet. It is also thanks to her that Nakala didn't come after you today with all his powers of divination. They know you took her by black magic because no one in their right mind would attempt such a thing in the dark without supernatural help. You have introduced a new form of deceit, have you not, no straight-forward magic about it but some English cunning, eh? "

"No! Our escape was totally straight-forward."

"Be that as it may, you will always have to watch out for Nakala—he bears grudges and will always be wary of you, but he does like the liquor too. Better give extra to please him. They'll get a taste for it, Lily, which is as disconcerting to me as my taste for good black tea. It is not a kind thing to cultivate such dependencies."

Margery's words and tone were not lost on Lily whose heart sank. It was at that moment she realized Margery was questioning how long she would be staying. Unable to answer, she clasped Mkumi's hand solemnly instead, thanking her. "Margery, please tell her that I did have some supernatural help. Ask if she can identify the statue, and advise me what to do with it now."

Mkumi gasped, visibly taken aback, as Lily handed her the statue. Turning it in her hands, Mkumi polished it reverently, then cackled as she spoke.

Margery interpreted. "She is amused, but only just. You were either foolish in your ignorance or else lucky. This fetish holds the spirit of Chief Zwem's grandmother, 'Hala—that means 'tooth' because she had protruding front teeth, nicely sharp when filed. She was not only a great sorceress but a very difficult character, spiteful and unpleasant. The only reason she may have been helpful to you is that she never had any use for her son, Zwem's father. Sometimes these grudges are extensive. She never had any use for Nakala either, so you definitely picked the right person, or spirit, shall we say? Mkumi will be glad to put her back for you—in fact, this would be a wise thing to do."

"I'd be grateful," said Lily, feeling humbled about her whole adventure, "but don't you think she'd like a place on this side of the river—with us?"

## 20.

Shiwezi brewed the beer for her wedding. Since stories had spread about this beer, about the raid and ultimate escape with Lily, the occasion would be well-attended; Shiwezi was making many pots full.

Lily in the traditional role of a female family member, helped her by tending the fire or by gathering wood. Her many forays into the forest were accompanied by the children, girls and boys, who showed her the good hardwood, and helped her carry it back. Over the days she learned their names, proudly pronouncing each one as often as possible. She was delighted that Margery had named many of the babies. She was curious about the Faung words Margery had picked—*Blessing, Sunshine, This One is Chosen.* But Margery laughed at her when she asked why she had chosen those particular names. "Let us christen the four boys Matthew, Mark, Luke and John. The girls are either Mary or Martha, take your pick. When the boys are older they won't help with making beer any longer. They will turn to hunting and fishing."

"Perhaps these boys will be different."

"Let's hope not," said Margery tersely, "or they will go seek their fortunes as servants for the colonialists, and forget that they are hunters. Forget their real names."

"What about the girls then?"

"I don't know about the girls. I want them to learn fishing at least. They are on their way to being expert potters, thanks to Mgamelele's instruction—she's about the best around and we have her with us!—But as a rule, they will stay insulated a bit longer than the boys."

"Insulated?"

"Yes, I'm talking about after the railroad comes through, and the bamboo and timbers from the forest taken. Why else would anyone want to go to all the trouble of building a track, and bringing over engines, rail-cars. They have found coal deposits near Lake Fitzpatrick. There is bound to be more for the taking up this way. Why else come all this way except to strip away everything for God, Queen and country."

"You are casting a bleak future. I can hardly picture a railroad coming anywhere near here."

"Then you should listen to the people down on the coast. Everyone knows that the Robolo is much too wild for navigation. They like to roll out their maps for you and show you where the railroad will go ."

"A dream on a paper doesn't necessarily mean they can build it—why the Robolo is full of ravines, the bridges alone would be prohibitive."

Margery looked at Lily with a derisive smile. "You will see. You come as a trader. You prove it is possible; next come the prospectors after coal deposits and gold. No one here will be satisfied with wholesome indigenous beer anymore. It'll be gin they want, the same stuff that keeps our own people poor and servile back home. I came from a poor parish, you know.

"My family was an oddity because there were only three of us children, and well fed, not the usual dozen running about in rags and filth, their parents drunk, the children neglected and beaten, either begging, pick-pocketing or working in the factories, because they were on the brink of starving. We treat our own like dogs—why will it be any different here? The fortune hunters will come. And I don't want my children being the cheap labor for them. You see a people here who were untouched by the slave snatchers in the past, because they are so far inland. Don't you see that you, as a trader, open the way for this kind of exploitation?"

"Not at all. Trading is as old as history the world over, Margery. For me it is a form of communication—a give and take, a reason to seek people out. And I am certainly not trading to put people in bondage."

"But in thinking of going back to England, what you are

164

proposing is some sort of trade route, and it is like exposing someone to a new disease—some life-line of liquor for Chief Zwem, pleasing or plying me with tea in the process. Why can't you just get some liquor at Nelson and Brodwick and be done with it?"

"At triple the price? I don't have the resources to carry on that kind of commerce."

"Take the money you brought me."

Lily sighed in frustration. "What I wanted to do was take Ngobi with me as far as the Trading Station. He could bring back cloth and enough tea to last you until I come back. And I will write to you. We can write to each other—I will leave you pen and paper. If you send Ngobi down river every few months, I will send letters to the Trading Station for him to bring to you."

"I have forgotten how to write," said Margery bitterly. "Besides it would take months for any letter to reach you."

"I only want to go back long enough to re-supply myself."

"That will take at least a year—oh look!" Margery turned away suddenly and deliberately as a stir of activity roused the villagers. "Here come the drummers all gleaming and in their finery. They will announce the wedding tonight and everyone will dance. You had best get back to the bride. You must keep vigil with her all night. The dance is for her but she may not see it. Off you go."

So Lily did, but her heart was heavy, her mind unsettled.

She went to sit in the marriage brewery like any female relative would do. 'Mgamelele and Mkumi brought Mtoli back and forth, brought food, and a beaded skirt for Shiwezi with a yellow band of 'co-wife' in between two thick lines of blue, but Margery did not come.

Lily tried to find some sleep and comfort on the mat in that hut, but she felt stiff and achy, the pain coming back in her head so that she thought she would choke. Or was it just the heavy stench of sweet, fermenting brew that assailed her? Was it the thick smoke that boiled out of the coals, filling the hut so that she could only gasp air when she lay down flat against the ground. It was as though the hut had become a great eyeless mask which she wore heavily over her head, a gigantic upside-down corset, and she was supposed to dance but could not take the steps for the heaviness, the powerlessness of her ignorance and difference. All the while, she menstruated heavily, aching there in the pit of her being.

Outside the drummers played. The forest resonated. She could feel the beats in the ground, the thud of bare feet on the hard-packed earth shaking the hut, loosening all variety of creatures from the thatch. The men were dancing; they danced for Ngobi's strength and virility as the groom.

Shiwezi, in contrast, remained silent, tending the fire, her hands forever busy, this time fashioning pots out of clay which she then put into a kiln of coals she had made for them to bake in. Once in awhile, Lily was able to crawl out and fetch more firewood from the big pile outside, and watch the dancers briefly, the shadows flickering against the hut walls in response to the fires burning. She thought she might see Margery, and call to her, but she did not see her at all. Probably she is with the children, putting them to sleep, or cuddling with them, and all the while the drummers play, thought Lily. Why won't she come to me? Has our love broken because of who and what we are, so that she must cast me aside in her distress, her displeasure with me?

Miserably, she went back into the hut. Again and again.

Mkumi came for a ritual partaking of the beer, her eyes bright berries in the flickering of the fire-light, the creases of her face deep with smiles in greeting. She came, not as a relative, but as an impartial judge, Mtoli at her breast, unhurried in handing him over to Shiwezi. Lily moved to make room for her as Shiwezi dipped a calabash in the pot, then handing it first to Lily. Perturbed, Lily took it and raised the bowl tentatively to her lips. How would she know whether it was good, or what it needed when she had not even learned to drink it yet. Mkumi laughed, gesturing for her to sniff it first, put a dab on her tongue, let it roll around. Lily laughed nervously back, and followed the instructions—a drop. She let it roll around on her tongue, and shrugged her helplessness. Giving Mtoli to Shiwezi, Mkumi took the bowl, dipped a finger in and sucked, flicking the excess away, grunting, shaking her head in approval, talking to Shiwezi—giving recommendations. Turning to Lily, she handed the calabash back and encouraged: taste it again. So Lily did, trying to get the idea as Mkumi pronounced the word for *good*. Lily nodded back and repeated the word, savoring the brew. As it sat on her tongue the bitterness became sweet. She could feel the flavor in her nose, flaring into her head, smiling in satisfaction now, and sipping more, so that Shiwezi clapped, pleased. Lily was learning.

The gourd made its rounds, Lily growing braver in her stupor, her dull resignation. And Mkumi began talking, Shiwezi humming in response. Lily strained to understand; it was a story but she could only catch bits and pieces. Something about a young maiden who found a magic brewing pot, but when the chief wanted to marry her, the contents turned sour—the story was delivered in explosive phrases, amid much laughter—because it was only the women who had grown drunk from it together. There had to be a message or advice in it all for her because Mkumi was direct, admonishing her. In matters of the heart, perhaps?—she kept saying a word, demonstrating the act of giving birth, hands rubbing her inner thighs, shaking her hips and laughing. Some word she repeated, but Lily didn't know the meaning.

Here was this great diviner whom Margery loved and respected, passing on her wisdom in her deep, melodious voice while Lily sat like an imbecile at her feet, remembering Margery's words: 'What?—do you think you'll gain a private audience with the Queen when you get home, a seat of honor at the table? She is no greater, I daresay, certainly not nearly as astute as Mkumi who walks about right in our midst. But then, I wonder if you can truly see that."

No, thought Lily ruefully, no; nor could I understand the language and the manners of my English Queen for that matter. I do know that I'd rather sit here on this grass mat, and share a bowl of Shiwezi's marriage brew, than be ushered in to curtsey in the presence of Victoria.

After Mtoli had nursed, Shiwezi gave him back to Mkumi who wagged her finger at Lily to keep tasting, keep tasting as she left.

Perhaps the beer had great properties because deep in the night, Lily finally became clear-headed. Or maybe it was because Shiwezi handed her a small lump of clay, wet and well worked so that it was pliable. No words, just a simple gesture. Slowly by the light of the glowing coals, Lily played with the clay until it seemed to be taking shape, starting out as a small bowl. She realized she had made the bowl of a pipe. Finding a piece of straw from the thatch, she made a hole in it, then fashioned a stem. She took great pains to smooth all the surfaces and edges. After it baked hard in the next days, and the piece of straw burned away, she knew Shiwezi would claim it from the ashes and give it to Margery. More importantly, she realized that Shiwezi had completed their own bonding as relatives, because they had touched each other along the way, at the heart of their suffering.

When the sun rose, Ngobi came up to the hut and chanted to his bride: *Is the beer ready?*

Shiwezi sang back shyly: *I have made the beer for my husband.*

Then Ngobi: *You have made me a man today and proud to offer beer to my guests. Come out, my bride, and greet me.*

His song was chorused by the villagers in bawdy refrains, their voices trilling with flirtation calls.

And Shiwezi came out.

Blinking at the daylight, Lily followed after her, attending her by bringing forth the beer. From among the throng of people, Mbo stepped forward to greet her, his lips wide across his filed teeth, saluting her cockily, "It is one hell of a picnicki!"

Lily laughed in spite of herself because she felt worn and at a loss. How she cherished him. She did not think he was ever one to feel sorry for himself.

Only then, as the wedding day feast took hold amid promises of wild hilarity and abandon, did Lily spy Margery standing in the courtyard holding up a pot of steaming tea, summoning with a nod of her head, as if they had barely parted.

"You didn't come to the bridal hut," Lily approached her accusingly, pent up emotions spilling out in her cutting tone.

Margery cocked her head slightly, smiled, "Of course not.

I have been standing by Ngobi. If Shiwezi is to come to this village, then it must be to come into his family. To stand by him as his 'mother' means that I may receive her. But it would be taboo for me to enter the bridal chamber. Do you see?"

Lily sighed, her self-indulgent dejection washing out of her as Margery handed her a cup of tea. "I don't know which ones you observe and which ones you don't."

"Whichever is convenient in a given situation. Therein lies the power as long as you can get away with it."

## 21.

"Come Lily," said Margery taking her hand, "let's to our mountain. Everyone is satisfied and busy now."

"If I can trust there won't be a raid," answered Lily, eager to retreat.

"Only over Ngobi's dead body."

"Don't say that."

Arms linked they made their way together, Margery shouldering a rolled up mat, until the path narrowed on the ascent and Lily fell in step behind her. The stinging sun gave way to the dark green cool of the giant trees covered with moss, glistening green and as thick as fur. Slowly the trees thinned and gave way to thickets of bamboo.

Lily had expected harmony between them now. But by the time they reached the emerald temple of bamboo, she realized the silence between them was not peaceful. The uneasiness was not just her own. There had been so much left unsaid while the festivities distracted them.

How could she leave? How could she stay? Before the wedding, such questions could be put off for another day, kept vague even while she negotiated with Chief Zwem over trade items, but now Shiwezi was married, the raid resolved.

They reached the summit, jumping from ledge to ledge until they reached Margery's favorite outcropping like the turret of some great roof where they could see the whole world.

Margery sighed, the etched lines about her eyes crinkling. "Here is my freedom, Lily. I live for this. Do you understand?"

Lily gazed out at the distant, smoky mountains, the river

which was too far away to hear, and nodded solemnly.

"Then smile, my darling, it should make you happy too."

"It does," Lily whispered back.

"My desires are very simple, you know." Margery reclined on the rock, extending an arm to pull Lily down against her. "As simple as wanting to share this with you." She played with Lily's hair, stroking it as Lily let her head sink into Margery's shoulder. "Why did you have to go fetch Shiwezi like that, so quickly? You had to be so expedient."

Lily's head lurched in response.

"No, don't move so sharply," Margery's open hand pressed Lily's head back to her shoulder. "You spurred time on. You will be telling me next that you must go. Do you think I don't know this? I have seen you wringing your hands, pacing about."

"Pacing about?" retorted Lily, "When? I have been lugging firewood."

"Ah, but I know—you brought back more than was needed. You are distressed, your mind going every which way—everywhere else but here."

Not true, Lily wanted to protest but it was true. "I'm torn, that's all."

"That's all? Lily...."

"I have a passage booked on the steamer, *Fair Trader,* which comes up from the Cape of Good Hope, and passes the coast here sometime in May. That gives me maybe six weeks to work my way down the Robolo, into Lake Fitzpatrick and the lower Oguye—if I am to make that embarkment. I have been measuring my time by it—give or take a few days—or weeks."

Margery pursed her lips. "Perhaps you don't have to measure time anymore, at all. Besides, you can make it down the river in a month unless you are trading extensively or exploring. But you have already found me, so what else can there be to do but enjoy what you have found?"

"Yes," Lily smiled wanly. "But barring fatal injury or disease, I was to be back for my brother's return from the Orient, or even before."

"Oh Lily," said Margery, bursting with annoyance. "Why

171

on earth do you have to be back just because he is? From what you have told me he is little more than a stranger. And what if he has met with a misadventure or missed his steamer—have you thought of that?"

"I can only do my part."

Margery smiled sadly then, and looked away to the horizon. A long silence was followed by, "Rushing home like a good English lady to take care of the man of the family. Hasn't Africa, haven't I, taught you anything?"

"That was the plan I had to make—my travels could not interfere with his return."

"Don't be daft—all that has changed! You are here. Will he come in search of you, drag you back to be his housekeeper? By God, I'd answer for you before I'd let any such raid happen. Come now, would he even contemplate such action?"

"No."

"Then why go at all when you are meant to be by my side?"

Lily did move away sharply at this, leaning on her knees to gaze out upon the heart of Africa. "I did not come to Africa with any intention of staying, but for adventure, to explore, to trade my way along. And I have been touched to my core, but I am a visitor, not a resident. I can't hope in my heart to be anything else, because I am the foreigner here. For you, it makes sense, I can see that—as if you had pledged loyalty to a new queen." She looked down ashamed of her dependence. "In any case, I have to be in England in person to claim my pittance of an inheritance or else the money will go without thought of my welfare into my brother's account. With it I will be able to come back.... But first, by going back, not only can I can bring further trade, and so re-finance myself, but also to enlighten our own people of what Africa truly is, teach them so that the colonialists who do come out inevitably, can come with a better appreciation and respect."

Margery spat. "Teach them respect? A hopeless task." She put a strong hand on Lily's shoulder. "Such noble talk! A waste of time. It will not change the opportunistic tide of people coming out. I can live and die with the Faung here out of respect. With my presence alone things have changed—and now with you. Why did you have to find me?"

In agony Lily bit her lip before speaking deliberately, painfully. "I cannot stay here now. I have to go back. Everything there tugs at me." She smiled sadly. "Even Audrey too, our cook—she was my real mother, if I can claim her. She expects me back. It doesn't mean I don't want to return, or that I find it easy to leave. This is where I want to come back to."

She touched Margery tenderly, looked into her grey eyes, wistfully. "You could come back with me for a time—we could find a cottage by the sea, where we can write, find like-minded people to converse with. And then we could always come back."

"Like-minded people! Who will care what you think? England holds nothing for me, Lily, even if I wanted it to. The Mission would give me all kinds of trouble and try and claim me back into their clutches somehow—on breach of contract! That alone makes me shudder. I am an indentured servant who escaped into the bush, presumably to perish! And really, I have no desire to travel, except on this continent—and only if I have to."

Lily groaned in frustration. "Have you lost all zest for adventure, Margery?"

"You call living in England adventure? Anyway, I have never seen my life in terms of adventure," Margery countered flatly, "but as a burden I struggled to get out from under—and this is where I ended up. You are still trying to shake yourself free—certainly I would not want you here unless it was willingly. I will go find the source of the Nile with you, if you like."

Lily hung her head between her knees, smothering her sharp breaths in her skirt. Slowly from behind, Margery's arms and legs enveloped her, a gentle voice coaxing her. "Shh, it's all right, Lily, we are bound freely in our love. We have to be. It doesn't matter where we are. Right now, you are with me—your body...And I have known all along you were a Visitation, did I not? Come, be with me, darling."

"But we are sad."

"Christmas never lasts long. Perchance, it comes again...."

Turning, flinging herself upon Margery who sank back against the rock in surprise, Lily gazed into her beloved's eyes for a long moment. "At least, won't you come to the coast with me?"

"To see you off? No, Lily, no. The people on the coast disgust me. The whites are cruel and they have already broken the spirits of the blacks there. I have made my choice—sometime ago. Don't forget that I have already gone back to see. I can't explain it for you—it is for you to go back and make your own choice. Obviously, you still feel an attachment. I thought I did too—to my country, to my Queen, for God's sake! All I found out is that one day when I was crossing the street something charged at me; I thought it was a hippopotamus, but it was an omnibus. Go, see. Then you must come back—I can only trust that you shall. You know where to find me." And she smiled then, her eyes alight with passion and tenderness so that Lily cried out, kissing her again, again.

"Yes, yes I will come back."

"I think it is very hard on this rock," said Margery suddenly. "Don't you think we could find a softer place?"

The best they could find was a crevice between two boulders, filled over time with earth and finally a layer of moss. Shadow from an overhanging tree promised to lengthen as the sun moved west. Lily unfurled the grass mat for them. "See, this is the mat I will take with me because I will know I was close to you then—always."

"Don't talk," said Margery, unbuttoning Lily's blouse, hands seeking out her breasts to stroke them gently, "we are on the mountain now." Pressing her moist lips against Lily's, she pushed her gently down. "In England, you know, there is only fear and constraint over love like this."

"It doesn't exist...." but Margery smothered Lily's words with her mouth, her tongue settling all their arguments; laughing in her throat as she played, Lily answering her movement.

"Of course it exists," said Margery when they stopped for a moment, breathless, "And you will not fail to so notice when you go back—but seldom with such joy and such ease, eh? Here there is a term for our love. It is the same word used for 'midwifery' but the intonation is different and means 'bring forth.' It expresses sensual affections, but also what you did for Shiwezi when you came out of the hut with her beer. All of it is connected."

Ah, so that was the word Mkumi had used in the hut over beer. Lily stroked Margery's hair, tucking the locks that fell forward, back behind her ears. "How do you know—did you—before you came here?"

"Perhaps I did in an unclear way. Remember my cousin who brushed my hair? That is as simple as our love was, but I certainly loved her. I used to plan to run away to somewhere with her. She said she would steal me away before the Mission sent me off that fateful day which was to arrive sometime after my twenty-first birthday. I went ahead with my training as a nurse. She worked in a factory and lived in an unheated attic with twenty other women. Meanwhile there was some question as to whether I shouldn't be sent out as someone's wife, but I caused a fuss over that—enough, so that my brother would serve as escort. Where were we going to go? How were we to live? Our letters and dreams kept us alive. But then, my dear cousin died of consumption. She had kept her sickness a secret from me. It was a great loss to me—she became ill when I was away in training—and then, what a dreadful day for me when I walked up the gangplank of the ship to leave. I went like a lamb, just like Shiwezi, and just as full of resolve, I see now. I did not know yet about my brother's desertion. He had gone ahead and was to meet me—only, he had gone to the Cape of Good Hope. I can't say that I cared much where I went, because I had lost—I had lost Nan..." Her cousin's name was the slightest whisper on her lips so that Lily barely understood. Margery kissed Lily as if to erase her memory. "I have not spoken her name in a long time. The first time I did in many years was with Mkumi. And she understood me—it all began with her touching my hair which was still long at the time. It was through Mkumi that I learned about physical affection in the first place, what 'laying on of hands' truly meant. I was used to many hands on me by then, but her hands were different, they said something different when they touched me—an acknowledgement, a respect. It was shattering—just to sense our similarities, and our differences. I was never the same after that—I broke free."

"I knew it," choked Lily, stiffening with jealousy, recognizing this way of being wounded. The way she had felt when Aunt Vanessa had let her go, had left her—an inexplicable pain. Now she knew she had felt it all her life—betrayal. Margery loved Mkumi. She had loved her cousin. More than she loved.... Lily couldn't hide the emotion in her voice as she said, "I could tell when Mkumi came back after dealing with Nakala how you felt about her. Is that why you stay?"

"Don't be a fool," Margery scolded, tightening her legs around Lily's hips and kissing her ear, arms cradling her. "Can't you see anything, ever? Mkumi and I are family, that is certain, but she alone is not the reason. Don't you see?—I have my children! They create tomorrow for me. I would wither away without them. To dust! Besides, she has grown very fond of 'Mgamelele who has refused marriage arrangements on her account. And I am not doing that, am I?"

"Refusing marriages?" And then Lily laughed, letting Margery's body sink into hers, Margery's hands running up her thighs, feeling once again how her skirt got in the way.

"Yes, when the village was raided, Mkumi thought they were coming for 'Mgamelele. Marriage for 'Mgamelele could only mean the lowliest position of abuse in a village because she is considered ugly due to her burn, never mind the laughter in her wide, doe eyes. She walked into a fire when she was very little. Mkumi laughs and calls her 'fire walker'— that she would dare such a thing at so young an age means she is strong against the shadows, and so, feared. She loves to watch the flame from a small lamp for hours." Margery sat up, and bracing herself against Lily's hip with her thighs, pulled off her tattered dress so that Lily could touch her muscular stomach, caress her breasts.

"You are like a magnificent fetish, towering so above me," said Lily, gazing up, Margery's face in shadow as her torso blocked the sun.

Working to loosen Lily's skirt, Margery snorted, "Then you

176

will know what to carve for me out of some pale wood when I die—breasts sagging down to my navel, a swollen mouth between my thighs which cries out for you. You will let bamboo grasses grow up around me because I am so terrible, so fearsome. Come now—let me see how I would carve you."

And her hands ran over Lily's skin as their bodies came together. Holding Lily's hips tightly against her own, Margery moved slowly at first. "Here is my mouth hungering for deep kisses from you." Lily moved, their legs entwining, then pressed her on into a long slow rhythm until their bodies worked in unison side by side in the cleft of the rock, flesh and blood, fluids and sweat, pulsing in recognition and longing. Their mouths and tongues found each other as the tension between them heightened, their hearts setting the beat. Sliding her hands between Lily's thighs, Margery shifted to bury her face there, saying, "Kisses for you, kisses for your swollen lips," like a song. Lily could feel billowing clouds within her, the way the storm had unfurled that night above the courtyard, boiling across the sky. A long time—boiling and boiling, until she could hear the very sound, a deafening roar inside her as Margery held her tighter, her tongue calling to her, calling again with urgency. Screaming in her throat, screaming in her womb, Lily shattered, answering.

"There, my sweet," Margery whispered in satisfaction, moving her lips to kiss Lily's neck and shoulders. "Cry out for me, cry out. Have I not brought you forth? Is that not what we do for each other?"

Drenched in sweat, Lily rasped, "Is it right to know this—to know this much?"

Margery laughed, their drenched bodies slipping apart as she leaned on an elbow, her fore-finger running along the bridge of Lily's nose. "If you don't write about it. You simply cannot write about this in your travelogue—hm?—for your like-minded people."

Lily pulled her down again. "Then I might as well not write anything about Africa at all."

"Might as well not. You will be misunderstood, ridiculed, or worse, shunned. I don't suppose you could leave me out of your narratives altogether, just write about the Faung—their habits are shocking enough. No one will believe you that Faung women know how to bring each other birth and pleasure all at the same time. No one will believe you when you state that a Faung man can hold his liquor as well as any drunken English sailor. Who do you think will be convinced that the Faung are content to live as subjects of the forest rather than as masters of it? If you do put me in, keep me civilized, won't you?—properly attired with my parasol and Bible, bringing God to the heathens, and subjects to their Queen."

"And be like Fitzpatrick? It was because of what he wrote that I came to see for myself...." she cradled Margery's head, then kissed her tenderly, full of passion as Margery's perspiration trickled onto her face. "No, no I couldn't do that. And I would never have been prepared for you—for any of this— had I not had a fine chunk of Africa to slog through first."

Margery gazed down into her eyes. "Would that you could give me another name! At least don't give particulars or details of my actual whereabouts."

"That I would never divulge."

"Disguise me as a man, say a prospector with his native wives and children, and yet, for all his uncouth ways, he treated you courteously, a fine gentleman." Head tilted up against the sky, Margery laughed nervously. "Write about a country rife with disease, pestilence, ignorance and evil, how these savage and rude people need linen towels and bandages, worn-out shoes and the alphabet. This is something that can be understood and accepted."

Was there a touch of fear in those sad grey eyes, Lily wondered. Eyes that were like the very mists of Britain, but with the sunlight longing to break through, luminous. Was she still afraid in the back of her mind that the Mission would try and reclaim her, take her back against her will—just like in a raid? For the first time Lily sensed the fragility in Margery, saw the hair-lined crack in her strength and defiance. Pushing her against the mat, Lily covered her with kisses.

## 22.

The time had come to settle with Mbo, Peta and Topi.
They had brought her safely to Shi Robolo, and her payment
was to uphold their coming-of-age as men worthy of marriage. She would give them a stock of bamboo-handled
scythes which were particular to the Robolo tribes, plus
bamboo fishing spears, all for trading purposes—and enough
to insure good bride-prices. She added liquor, tobacco and
clay pipes for their pleasure, and gave each a three-inch
steel-bladed expedition knife. They valued the last items
above all the others; she had known they would, Mbo having
always admired the one she carried, and had kept them in
reserve for this occasion.

Now the men brandished them with pleasure, showing
the children how the sharp point of the knife could draw
blood, and how well it could carve into wood.

She was touched when Mbo questioned shyly whether she
needed an escort down the river. He wanted to be sure she
found her husband. But she assured him that Ngobi, and
others from the local area would see her that far. He didn't
argue but shook his head agreeably, saying yes, and it was
time for him to go home. Time to find his wife and grow in
wealth! But his reluctance over his departure echoed her
own—he traded meat for a source of beer and took the opportunity to have one more night of drinking and dancing,
and one more day of sobering up, before he shouldered his
goods along with his companions, and bade farewell.

Gently, Lily touched the extra amulet he wore around his
neck, remembering the burden of Masa that he carried home
with him. Then with his wide smile that had often encour-

179

aged her along the way, he departed, singing the song of journey and parting ways, Peta and Topi providing the refrain, until the forest enveloped him.

Had she not walked with him, eaten his game and lived with him more closely and with more feeling than she had ever lived with her own blood? Hadn't her very survival depended on him? How could she let him go like that with no expectation of seeing him again?

In her heart it wasn't so simple, because it meant it was time for her to organize her own departure. As she sat in Margery's hut consolidating her packs into a much lighter load, she wondered at the folly of her plan.

It didn't help that Margery came and went cheerfully with the children about her, close on the surface but distant on deeper levels. Lily felt her friend to be waiting—waiting to see, waiting for the parting to be done.

They still slept under the mosquito netting together at night, almost forgetting that they weren't one, but the passion Lily had experienced on the last trip to the mountain seemed to have stayed up there as if Margery had made a statement, an argument, and had given up the discussion with Lily's answer.

Then, on the last night when Mbo and the others lolled about drinking and recounting their adventure, she said one more time, "Stay with me, Lily."

Lily was in despair. The silence hung about them almost as if Africa herself reproached her. She was rescued for a moment by a rustling in the rafters, a movement. She threw her head back, eyes staring wide up at the thatch, happy for even the slightest distraction.

Then finally she forced herself to say. "I cannot live here like you do. You have your work here. Mine is not here. You know that we cannot be free to each other if we are not each free within ourselves as well. I have negotiated a trade with Chief Zwem. For clay and bamboo I can bring back knives, fish-hooks, cotton, and yes, liquor. With the women I can trade glass beads for woven mats and pottery. And then there will come a time when I will no longer be beholden to my brother or tied by family money.

Her voice grew stronger in the silence. "I cannot remain isolated—nor should you. If anything I must come and go. I am not in exile, and I have unfinished business with my own people. There are things I want to tell them. Here I can leave no mark, but in England I can be of influence about the issues of contact with Africa. This is what I want."

Margery snorted. "I am not isolated. It is only that we are both strong-willed." There was an impatience in her voice now, the pleading gone. "I wish I could spare you going back to those you suppose are your people. But then you hardly know them, really. It's as though you never knew them to begin with. What good was your intelligence then? You will never be accepted the way you want, no matter how many books you write. You will be seen as something exotic,  amusing but.... Here is where you belong. You have a place even though you hardly have a command of the language yet. You...."

Another rustle above silenced her or perhaps she simply gave up. In the dim lamp-light of the hut, Lily sat up in alarm to inspect what creature moved up there, six feet above them. "My god, Margery?—do you see?" She whispered hoarsely. "Isn't that a snake?"

Margery sat up slowly as an elongated form wound its way in and out of shadow, glowing in the dim lamp-light as it slipped across the rafter. "Oh, yes, she comes and goes like you shall. There the similarity ends, I suppose. She is of a poisonous variety, you see, and she hunts mice up there in the grass. I am glad to see her winding her way along because then I know she won't drop. She did once but she has learned. She was moving flat along the beam when suddenly, plop, she landed right on my belly. She must have been extremely frightened or embarrassed, or perhaps she was after a mouse that had fallen too because she was gone in an instant—a bolt of muscle across me before I even had time to complain. We are at peace, she and I."

Lily reached out a tentative hand. "And pray, so may we be."

Margery touched her shoulder, pulling her back gently. "I am not afraid of that snake, see?—I am afraid of losing you,

181

afraid that you will be ensnared upon your return to England. It is so dangerous. Beware, beware of all those duties lacing up the corset of your money. Oh, the journey itself is nothing. I would rather let you go up and down the Robolo over and over, than know you are going back to England. It is not that I don't believe you want to come back to me—it is that anything can happen to us. Before I did not know of you, but now I do—I must relearn about living without you here and it is a hard thing. It must not be that I ever catch myself waiting for you."

"My loyalty is to you," said Lily solemnly, "that is my oath to you."

Margery buried her face against Lily's breasts. "Please don't make me promises that you might find you simply cannot keep."

In the early morning light, Lily sat on one of the packs facing out the open doorway of the hut, the veil of frayed gauze billowing in. She needs new mosquito netting, Lily brooded, I will send some back up with Ngobi. I will send some cotton too, and leave her a set of clothes to tide her over—oh, she won't wear the skirt for long anyway, will she?—when all she wants is the efficiency of pantaloons.... I should bring her a pair of men's trousers perhaps. They would be more comfortable. Perhaps she would be wearing a beaded skirt when I come back, she thought, amused by the image.

Sitting chin in hand, she thought back on the woman who had left England. It was as if she were another, an alien being. She could no longer remember the feelings that had brought her to this land as a trader in the first place. She thought of Margery's statement, "It was my god-forsaken destiny."

When she had come to Africa, it had been for herself. And she had ended up searching for another woman, another Englishwoman instead, and had lost her heart.

Now, in her new nakedness, how could she go out into the world she had known, clothed again? —corseted? Would she become bound up again as Margery warned? Would she become that other woman again?

She smiled to herself. Somehow she knew she was really changed, that she could go back without losing this new self. Would she think an omnibus was a hippopotamus when she tried to cross a street?

Had she really cracked a primordial silence by firing her revolver in the rain forest? Twice.

How could she ever live with doors, locks and bolts again?

How could she stop this tide within herself that told her to go, to go further? How could Margery ever doubt that she would come back here?

She remembered Masa whose drum she carried—why had the leopard sprung upon him, the man going just ahead her? If it had chosen a later moment, she would never have found Miss P.

How had she really indebted herself to Chief Zwem for liquor?—out of loyalty to Shiwezi? Toying with the copper bracelet on her arm, she thought about Shiwezi a long time, this woman she had met by chance, their lives having become interwoven like the strands of grasses in a mat. Somehow she very much liked the fact that she was indebted now to Chief Zwem. It was like the hidden key to anything that might lock her up back in England, because she would have to come back and repay her part. Couldn't Margery understand that?

Most of all, she came round again and again to the saddening thought of how she was ever really going to boat down the Robolo, away. Away.

A movement in the courtyard roused her. It was Margery returning without the children, her brisk, un-African stride the one, very English thing that stubbornly clung to her. With a few steps, she shadowed the door, pushing aside the netting as she ducked in, face to face with Lily.

"Waiting for the boat, are you? The Fair Trader? A patience in you, sitting there so independent and alone in the world."

"Patience?" Lily scoffed, but did not move. "What I have cultivated is endurance with a calm exterior, that's all. I learned it at my mother's knee, so to speak."

"Yes, and I admire that in you—I have never travelled the way you do, forging ahead. I was always moving away from something, desperately, severing bonds as I went until I came to rest here, while you deny nothing of what you are— your country, your heritage. You want to improve on it. Why, you have more missionary zeal than I have ever had." With an open gaze, she slipped an arm around Lily's waist, coming to sit slightly behind her on the pack. Leaning on Lily's shoulder, she whispered, "Lily, darling, bring me real china cups for my tea. I always wanted real china. Some that isn't cracked or chipped."

"You might as well be asking me to carry a calabash of beer across the ridges of a crocodile's back without spilling a drop." Lily tilted her head back, feeling Margery's hair against her temple and ear.

Margery laughed in her throat, almost a snort, tightening her arm around Lily, her hand spreading wide across her stomach. "You learned that from the story of N'ngia who mistook a crocodile for a log when he was on his way to deliver the secret beer—which incidentally, he had stolen from the women—to give the men. And explains why the women still brew the beer to this day."

"Yes; even so, my statement still applies."

"But you will find a way, Lily. You can carry liquor bottles quite effectively."

"Don't bring up the subject of liquor." Lily stiffened, defensively.

"Shh. No, no. I have another request of you."

Lily shifted, trying to see if Margery was serious.

"How can I entreat you to stay away from Greely Mission on my behalf. If you go there, you will be pointedly questioned. And you will not be able to say you have not seen me."

Taking Margery's chin and turning it towards hers, Lily answered, "I give you my word."

"You know, if you send me letters, they will end up there. I will never get them. I cannot guarantee they won't be opened and read either."

"No, I will send any letters through Captain Lowell and he

will make certain to put them in with the post that goes to the Trading Station."

"Captain Lowell?" Margery smiled faintly. "Yes. He was the one who sent you here, after all. Yes, I suppose that would do, but you never know."

"I will send you Bible verses, underlined. Better yet, I will call you the source of my Nile, the well-spring of everything I am becoming from hence forth."

"The source of your Robolo, you mean." And then Margery kissed her, muffling her laugh, "Some sort of cipher!" Her eyebrows raised playfully.

They made light of any pain between them as their lips met, entering into a kind of conversation, a give and take, almost sharp at first, clipped and testing, their kiss rounding out then until their tongues met in open recognition. They believed in each other. They spoke more deeply together in that kiss than they could with any words. They made the promises that could not be spoken.

Slowly, Margery drew away, catching her breath. "Please don't take too long or I shall surely die of fever."

"I won't." Lily pulled her close again. She could feel that Margery was shaking. "I shall have to trust that Mkumi won't let that happen to you."

"Then I can let you go."

*I am terrified,* Lily wrote in her journal, the nib of her pen worn and scratchy, the ink in its bottle already watered down to a paler hue. *How can I go now and leave her? Leave someone who is my soulmate—if I am ever to claim that I have one? It is not that she and I are so similar; it is that she talks with me, gives me everything. I feel strong with her. I feel like the lion on the escarpment above that awful swamp— triumphant, even in the simple greeting of the day. It is because I can proclaim that I am.*

*I simply cannot deny my birth-right and my homeland yet. Will I find it as empty as I did the French mission on the Oguye? If anything, now I must prove that what M says is not so.*

\* \* \*

185

Lily went with offerings of fruit and a plug of tobacco to place at the feet of the statue of 'Hala on its new pedestal of stones behind the village. She half-hoped she might find a lively shadow beckoning to her, entreating her to stay, half fearing that it might. But nothing happened as she stood there arranging her gifts in farewell.

Hearing movement behind her, she turned to see Mkumi, 'Mgamelele, Shiwezi and Margery approaching. In Mkumi's hands was a small statue made out of blond wood with long, suggested tresses darkened with soot.

"See, we have made a twin statue of you out of ranga wood so that you shall never really leave. We shall give her food and a place of respect in your absence," Margery explained, "as is the custom when people of importance journey afar. You will notice the eyes are not like those of the dead."

Lily watched, checking her tears as Mkumi placed the statue next to that of 'Hala, on the same pedestal. How oddly African it look, carved in the Faung style, with wide lips and nose, seeds set in for the eyes, reminding her of the albino woman she had met, except for the long dark hair, and the suggestion of a hat. Nor did she fail to notice the statue's nakedness, the breasts that looked like buttons, and the swollen lips of power below the navel. She sputtered in laughter at her image there, wiping her eyes, sniffling, "Yes, she who knows little but finds her way."

"Has her way," corrected Margery, tracing with a finger over the round breasts. "I had to describe your breasts to Mkumi—it is extremely odd, you know, that I had to."

Lily reddened as she looked at the three pairs of dark eyes that studied her so frankly. Fumbling, she unfastened her blouse and removed it. A long sigh of approval enveloped her: Hm mmm, yes it is so, her breasts are round. And without ado, the women touched her, their fingertips appraising her as they clucked. Under their scrutiny, Lily gave up her shame, and laughed, her own hands touching their breasts boldly in return like a greeting back and forth and all around, from Shiwezi's still swollen with milk, 'Mgamelele's firm ones—the right one seared with burn scars, to Mkumi's leathery ones hidden among her many medicinal pouches of all sizes—a many-breasted woman. And Margery slipped her top off too until there was clapping and laughter, much jig- gling and bouncing of breasts, much shaking and showing off, Mkumi ululating so that the birds shrieked in the tossing trees above them.

"Do you understand?" queried Margery.

"Yes, they say what a pity, what a pity...."

"What a pity that women 'of the fish' cover their breasts. How the children must cry out to be fed. Come now, you must be off while the shadows are still held in check—it is the way. Put your shirt on. You shall need it where you are going."

"Yes," countered Lily, pointing to the statue, "but I'll know she doesn't have to."

* * *

The Robolo was swift and swollen from rain in the hills. The canoes along the bank swayed and bobbed in agitation; the crocodiles took to clinging upon rock islands and sand bars.

"You will make excellent time until the first portage," said Margery, shading her eyes as she contemplated the river.

Already singing, Ngobi was lashing Lily's portmanteau se- curely into the canoe as Lily watched. His admonishments to the river spirit were answered by a refrain the women and children sang, building a momentum. The children broke off in excited laughter. For them, Lily's careful embarkment made for good sport. Gingerly, she grinned as she found her balance, and nodded to Ngobi. Four other canoes were al- ready turning into the current, maneuvered by giddy young warriors, eager to take on the rapids down river, and dash themselves against the rocks. Otherwise, they were along to aid in Lily's venture to Nelson and Brodwick Ltd. on the north side of Lake Fitzi-patriki.

Ngobi held the canoe close to the bank with his paddle as Margery reached out to clasp Lily's hand. "Better you find a woman companion there in England, and live together in a cottage by the sea."

Locked in the grip of those deep grey eyes, darkly rimmed,

187

Lily answered firmly, "Better you not get the fever."

And then Margery let go, ever so simply, a twitch to her eyebrows. Ngobi pushed the canoe out onto the current, startling Lily into finding her balance. Shiwezi called out to him in farewell, the children jumping up and down, singing the river song: *swift as the fish we swim the rolling Robolo, brash as the crocodile we take on the rolling Robolo.*

Quickly, Lily turned her head to look back at one retreating figure in particular—one dressed in a cotton shirt already missing its buttons, and a pin-striped skirt. A singular woman soon to be engulfed by the great, green forest which leaned out to press against the current.

She heard herself call out urgently across the rush of water, "I will bring you tea in a china cup."

Rebecca Béguin has lived in Vermont for over fifteen years (those roots she always wanted), works with New Victoria Publishers, lives on and helps run a sheep farm. Recently she took up horse riding, and ice hockey with a great group of women (sure helps get through the winters). For seven years she has taught a world-ecology curriculum to young children. She thrives on African music which becomes more and more available in the U.S.

Other books by the author:
Her Voice In the Drum
Runway at Eland Springs

# Other Titles Available

## Mystery/Adventure by Sarah Dreher

**A Captive in Time** ($9.95 )ISBN-0-934678 22-7  Stoner finds herself inexplicably transported to a small dusty town in the Colorado Territory, time 1871 —and can't find a phone to call home!

**Stoner McTavish**  ($7.95) ISBN-0-934678-06-5 Ooriginal Stoner McTavish mystery. Msychic Aunt Hermione, partner Marylou, and Stoner, in the Grand Tetons rescuing dream lover Gwen.

**Gray Magic**($8.95) ISBN-0-934678-11-1 Stoner's friend Stell falls ill with a mysterious disease and Stoner finds herself an unwitting combatant in the great struggle between the Hopi Spirits of good and evil.

**Something Shady** ($8.95) ISBN-0-934678-07-3 Stoner travels to Maine with her lover Gwen and risks becoming an inmate in a suspicious rest home to rescue a missing nurse.

## Adventure/Romance

**Mari**  ($8.95) ISBN-0-934678- 23-5 The story of the evolving relationship of Mari, a woman who is an Argentinian political activist, and Judith, a New York musician.

**Dark Horse** by Frances Lucas ($8.95 ) ISBN-0-934678--21-9 Fed up with corruption in local politics, lesbian Sidney Garrett runs for mayor.

**As The Road Curves** by Elizabeth Dean ($8.95)ISBN-0-934678-17-0 Ramsey had it all; a great job at a prestigious lesbian magazine, and a reputation of never having to sleep alone. Now she takes off on an adventure of a lifetime.

**All Out** by Judith Alguire ($8.95) ISBN-0-934678-16-2 Winning a gold medal at the Olympics is Kay Strachan's all-consuming goal—until a budding romance with a policewoman threatens her ability to go all out for the gold.

**Look Under the Hawthorn** by Ellen Frye ($7.95) ISBN-0-934678-12-X A stonedyke from the mountains of Vermont, Edie Cafferty sets off to search for her long lost daughter and, on the way, meets Anabelle, an unpredictable jazz pianist looking for her birth mother.

**Runway at Eland Springs** by ReBecca Béguin ($7.95) ISBN-0-934678-10-3 While flying supplies into the African bush, Anna finds herself in conflict with a game hunter, and turns for love and support to Jilu, the woman at Eland Springs.

**Promise of the Rose Stone** by Claudia McKay ($7.95) ISBN-0-934678-09-x Mountain warrior Isa is banished to the women's compound in the living satellite, Olyeve, where she and her lover, Cleothe, plan an escape.

## Humor

**Cut Outs  and Cut Ups** — A Fun'n Games Book for Lesbians by Elizabeth Dean, Linda Wells, and Andrea Curran ($8.95)—ISBN-0-934678-20-0 Games, puzzles, astrology —an activity book for lesbians with hours of enjoyment.

**Found Goddesses:Asphalta to Viscera** by M. Grey & J. Penelope ($7.95) ISBN-0-934678-18-9 *"Found Goddesses is wonderful! All of it's funny, some inspired. I've had more fun reading it than any book in the last two years."* —Joanna Russ

**Morgan Calabresé; The Movie** N. Leigh Dunlap ($5.95) ISBN-0-934678-14-6 Wonderfully funny comic strips. Politics, relationships, and softball as seen through the eyes of Morgan Calabresé.

## Short Fiction/Plays

**Secrets** by Lesléa Newman ($8.95) ISBN 0-934678-24-3 The surfaces and secrets, the joys and sensuality and the conflicts of lesbian relationships and herstory are brought to life in these stories by the author of *A Letter to Harvey Milk* and *Good Enough to Eat*.

**Lesbian Stages** by Sarah Dreher ($9.95) ISBN-0-934678-15-4 *"Sarah Dreher's play scripts are good yarns firmly centered in a Lesbian perspective with specific, complex, often contradictory (just like real people) characters."* —Kate McDermott

**The Names of the Moons of Mars** by Patricia Roth Schwartz ($8.95) ISBN-0-934678-19-7 In these stories the author writes  humorously as well as poignantly about our lives as women and as lesbians. Winner of the Lambda Literary Award.

**Order from New Victoria Publishers, P.O. Box 27, Norwich, Vt. 05055**